"I never told you

Kim smiled. "Never. I would remember because I'd have been crushed."

Jax shifted his gaze to the fire. "Apparently I have a high tolerance for awful annoyances."

"So you're okay with me being here?"

He watched the fire without speaking.

"Jax?" she coaxed. "Did you hear me? Are you okay with me being here?"

"Sure," he said quietly. He glanced at her and nodded, his smile brief but as welcome as the fire's warmth. "Of course."

"I'm glad." She laid her head on his shoulder and closed her eyes.

Jax sat motionless, almost not breathing. Kim's scent coiled around him. Her breasts, pressed against his arm, burned seductively. Steeling himself, he glared unseeing into the fire. She stirred and sighed, the slight, throaty sound piercing his heart. Gritting his teeth on a curse, he distanced himself from her before he did something unforgivably stupid.

Renee Roszel has been writing romance novels since 1983 and simply loves her job. She likes to keep her stories humorous and light, with her heroes gorgeous, sexy and larger-than-life. She says, "Why not spend your days and nights with the very best!" Luckily for Renee, her husband is gorgeous and sexy, too!

Renee Roszel loves to hear from her readers. Send your letter and SAE to: P.O. Box 700154, Tulsa, Oklahoma 74170, U.S.A. Or visit her Web site at www.ReneeRoszel.com

Books by Renee Roszel

Don't miss any of our special offers. Write to us at the following address for information on our newest releases.

Harlequin Reader Service
U.S.: 3010 Walden Ave., P.O. Box 1325, Buffalo, NY 14269
Canadian: P.O. Box 609, Fort Erie, Ont. L2A 5X3

JUST FRIENDS TO...
JUST MARRIED

Renee Roszel

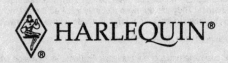

TORONTO • NEW YORK • LONDON
AMSTERDAM • PARIS • SYDNEY • HAMBURG
STOCKHOLM • ATHENS • TOKYO • MILAN • MADRID
PRAGUE • WARSAW • BUDAPEST • AUCKLAND

If you purchased this book without a cover you should be aware
that this book is stolen property. It was reported as "unsold and
destroyed" to the publisher, and neither the author nor the
publisher has received any payment for this "stripped book."

To my mother, Lenore Roszel,
My friend, confidante, sounding board and biggest fan.
I love you and miss you.

ISBN 0-373-03865-8

JUST FRIENDS TO...JUST MARRIED

First North American Publication 2005.

Copyright © 2005 by Renee Roszel Wilson.

All rights reserved. Except for use in any review, the reproduction or
utilization of this work in whole or in part in any form by any electronic,
mechanical or other means, now known or hereafter invented, including
xerography, photocopying and recording, or in any information storage
or retrieval system, is forbidden without the written permission of the
publisher, Harlequin Enterprises Limited, 225 Duncan Mill Road,
Don Mills, Ontario, Canada M3B 3K9.

All characters in this book have no existence outside the imagination of
the author and have no relation whatsoever to anyone bearing the same
name or names. They are not even distantly inspired by any individual
known or unknown to the author, and all incidents are pure invention.

This edition published by arrangement with Harlequin Books S.A.

® and TM are trademarks of the publisher. Trademarks indicated with
® are registered in the United States Patent and Trademark Office, the
Canadian Trade Marks Office and in other countries.

www.eHarlequin.com

Printed in U.S.A.

CHAPTER ONE

IN A state of shock, Kimberly sank to her knees in the middle of her empty condo. "This can't be happening. He can't be gone. I thought…" Her words faded into nothingness. Clearly she thought wrong. Her boyfriend of two years, the man she'd believed to be "the one," had moved out, taken everything.

From her vantage point on the cold wood floor, in the middle of what once was their living room, she amended the "everything" part. He hadn't taken quite everything. The gifts she gave him over the past two years lay in a neat pile nearby. The sports shirts, the half-used bottles of cologne, even the silk boxers covered in red hearts she bought one Valentine's Day when she felt a little wicked.

She noticed absently that he had left the two landscape prints on the wall that she had bought when a local furniture store had closed down. Numb, she scanned the pile of rejected gifts and noticed a folded sheet of paper sticking out from beneath one of the cologne bottles. The handwriting was Perry's. "If it says you've moved out, sweetheart, it was a waste of paper. I get the message." She swallowed around the lump in her throat, praying there was a good explanation in that note. Foolish, fleeting hope swelled in her heart with the fantasy that it would read, *Honey, I've been transferred to Paris.*

Couldn't reach you. Follow me soonest! Love, Perry. "And I bet there's a P.S. that says, *Didn't have room in my suitcase for these treasures. Please bring them.*" With great reluctance, she unfolded the sheet of notebook paper, muttering to herself, "Dream on, Kimberly."

She sat on her feet, terribly uncomfortable. But when a person drops to the floor in shock, comfort isn't the first consideration. Now, with pain shooting through her arches, she shifted her legs out in front of her, her slim skirt not giving her many options. With trembling hands, she smoothed the paper on a thigh. Hesitant to read the words she knew were there, she smoothed it several more times.

She'd come home from her trip so pumped up, so full of good news, with big plans to celebrate. Her fledgling career as a professional meeting planner took a big step forward today. After the unblemished success of the chiropractor's conference in Las Vegas she'd organized, she'd landed a big client, the owner of a chain of hardware stores. He'd hired her to plan his company's next corporate confab for January. That left plenty of time for a well-deserved vacation.

So, tonight she'd envisioned a quiet dinner, just the two of them, romantic candlelight, a little wine, and for dessert, making love on the rug in front of a crackling fire.

She glanced at the brick hearth, empty and cold and gray with soot, and blinked back tears. The only thing that would lie naked in front of it tonight would be the bare floor. She forced herself to look at Perry's note, to focus, read.

"You'll probably hate me for doing it this way," it began, "but you shouldn't be surprised. We've had the debate often enough. Face it, Kim, you're commitment phobic. I wanted marriage, but for two years you put me off. Well, I've had it. I've found somebody who isn't afraid to commit. Good luck with your life." It was signed, simply, "Perry." He added what looked like a hastily scrawled postscript which read, "Besides, I'll never measure up."

Miserable and baffled, Kim murmured, "Never measure up? What do you mean?" Her voice quavered with tears. "Measure up to what—to whom?"

She stared at the cryptic sentence, wiping away tears. After a long, silent struggle to get her mind around the ragged hole that had been shot through her life, she lifted her gaze to take in the gaping void that so suddenly shrouded everything. Perry's abandonment was a painful lesson of how little she'd given to their life together, at least materially.

"But…but I did care for you!" She picked up her favorite of his colognes and spritzed the air, inhaling. All at once, there Perry stood. Tall, blond, athletic, grinning that smirky grin that made her go gooey inside. Amazing about scents, the way they could conjure up a human being with only a few molecules of biochemical extracts. Suddenly disturbed by the smirking image, she waved her hand through the mist, trying to disperse the scent and erase him from the room. She succeeded only in perfuming her fingers. "I don't think I'll ever be able to stand that smell again," she muttered, wiping her hand on her linen skirt. "You reek, Perry," she said. "You lousy coward."

She didn't want to believe anything in his note had the slightest ring of truth. Commitment phobic? Not a bit. True, they did discuss marriage several times. She'd patiently explained she wasn't ready. She didn't like fighting, and never let one of their marriage discussions escalate to an argument. But even so, each time they "discussed" it, she pulled away a little more. Couldn't they simply be the compatible couple they were, enjoying the same movies, the same music, the same Chinese restaurant? Why did he have to rock the boat? He knew disagreements upset her.

Anger destroyed.

Hadn't she seen it enough with her mom, who spent Kim's formative years committing serial marriage? Her mother brought five husbands into their middle class tract house, interspersed by a few not-quite-so-committed boyfriends. Each of those relationships had been briefly happy, too soon deteriorating to volatile and unsettling. She grew to hate fighting, so the more Perry harried her, the more resistant she became.

She took in a shuddery breath, caught his scent and made a sour face. Glancing back at his note, she reread the postscript. "Besides, I'll never measure up."

"Measure up?" she whispered, as though trying to get a handle on what Perry meant. "Measure up?" She shook her head, bewildered. Hunched there, in the gathering darkness, her mind took her back, way back, to her next door neighbor, her best friend for all her growing-up years, Jaxon Gideon. Jax was three years older than Kim. He'd always been tall, even as a youngster. Since she couldn't count on a loving father in her life, Jax was the guy she ran to, blubbering, when she scraped her knee. And later, in high school, she still ran to him when a boyfriend dumped her, or even when she dumped a boyfriend, and simply felt down and alone.

Jax was also the guy she went to when she won something, like a class spelling bee, or the time she got her picture in the paper for writing the best essay in a city-wide contest on the topic, "Why I love St. Louis's Gateway Arch." Her mother was so busy cooing and panting over her latest husband she didn't even notice. But Jax was genuinely happy for her, even though he'd entered the contest, too. Of course, Jax was a science and math brain, which she never was, so their relationship never got competitive.

Childhood memories filled with Jax flashed by. She experienced a spark of warmth in her cold, desolate heart. Funny, but Jax had such a special place in her life that even thinking of him soothed her tattered spirit. She could hardly believe she'd let herself get out of touch with him over the past decade. Decade? Could it really be that long?

Well, she blamed Jax. After all, didn't she still live in St. Louis? He was the one who left to attend Northwestern University in Evanston, a suburb of Chicago, where he had stayed. Of course, they were grown-ups now. He had his life to live and she had hers. Their paths inevitably had to diverge. Which, to Kim, was a sad thing. She could use Jax living next door right now.

Back in high school, she'd sensed he had a crush on her. They went on a few dates, but Kim resisted a romance. She didn't dare put Jax into the "boyfriend" category. A person could lose a boyfriend, and Jax had been the only stable friend and confidant she'd known in her life. Her mother's many marriages, with all the fighting and the breaking up, scarred her. She hated upheaval so Jax became her rock, her comfort and solace. For that reason, she kept their dating casual and occasional, terrified that upping him to boyfriend status would throw him into the realm of chaos, where she spent too much of her young life. She couldn't risk it.

"I wonder what Jax is doing these days?" After graduating from Northwestern he started up a dot.com, made a bundle and got out before the bubble burst. She didn't know what he was doing now. Some kind of consulting, she'd heard, still in Chicago.

The last time she saw him was when her engagement to Bradley ended. Jax was in his third year at Northwestern, and she'd just started at a local junior college. Thinking her life was over, she fled to him and, as usual, he consoled her, told her it was "for the best," which, in hindsight, couldn't have been more true. Like magic, Jax got her back on track. After a week of crying on his broad, capable shoulders, she returned to St. Louis, into the chaos that ebbed and flowed through her world, leaving Jax solidly in his essential "friend" status.

She sniffed and swiped at a tear as she scanned the emptiness again. Her misery began to mutate into anger. Sucking in a shuddery breath, she cried, "How could you, Perry? How could you sneak out of our relationship like a thief in the night?"

All of a sudden she had a brainstorm. The shock of finding Perry gone had to be the worst disaster in her life to date. If she ever needed Jax, it was now. "That's absolutely what I need! *My Jax Fix!*" Not only would talking to Jax make her feel better, he would be happy for her when he found out about how well her business was doing. They could laugh and talk and...well, it would be like the good old days.

Before she knew she'd even moved, she grabbed her cell phone from her handbag and dialed directory assistance. She cleared her throat, struggling to sound like she wasn't on the verge of hysteria. "Hello—" Her voice cracked and she cleared her throat again. "I'd—uh—like the phone number of Jaxon Gideon in Chicago."

When she got it, she dialed. In her anticipation, a little of the ponderous sadness loosened its grip around her heart. The phone rang once, twice, three times, then a message came on. "Jaxon Gideon is unable to come to the phone. Please leave a brief message after the beep and he will return your call."

She managed a tremulous smile at the comforting familiarity of his baritone voice. His message was short and to the point, too. Nothing frilly or cutesy for Jax. She only hoped she could make it through her message without bursting into tears. "Hi, Jax," she began, almost in a whisper. "Guess who!" She shook her head at herself for the childish silliness. She laughed out of embarrassment. It sounded odd in her ears, a melancholy, almost a puppy whine of a noise. "Sorry. I won't make you guess. It's been way too long," she said solemnly. "It's Kim. Look, I—" She broke off, hesitating, unsure of how long her voice would hold out before it broke. "In all honesty, I could use a friend right now." She stopped, grimaced, facing facts. A phone call simply wouldn't be enough. "On second thoughts, I'm coming to see you." She congratulated herself on her brilliant idea. "I've gone way too long without my Jax Fix." She smiled to herself, amazed that she even could. It was Jax. All Jax, making her smile. "Okay, then," she said, feeling less like her emotional destruction had been total. "I'll see you soon."

She hung up and scrambled off the hard floor. "Jax Fix, here I come!" She headed for the entry where she'd dropped her suitcase, then stopped, twisted around and grabbed up the pile of Perry's cast-off shirts. In a fit of pique, she threw them into the fireplace. "They'll make perfect kindling for my next fire," she muttered. Hurrying into the entry she hoisted the suitcase she'd so recently lugged in. "Meanwhile, I'm catching the first flight to Chicago."

Jax was dog-tired when he got in from his long, tedious client dinner. Sometimes being a business productivity consultant reaped great rewards, both monetary and emotional. Other times, like tonight, it was like pulling teeth to get a company CEO to believe him when he outlined all they needed to do to increase productivity.

"He wants my expertise, but he doesn't want to hear what I'm saying." He shrugged out of his suit jacket and tossed it on the muted green suede sofa, then headed upstairs to his bedroom. Loosening his tie, he noticed his answering machine blinking. Strange. Everybody knew his cell number and left voice mail. He didn't even know why he still had the antiquated answering machine and land line. The truth was, he hadn't had the time to get rid of them.

Though he figured it was a telemarketer or a solicitation for donations, he pressed the button to hear the message. The instant he heard that voice, he froze in the act of pulling his tie from around his neck.

It was Kim.

After all these years of getting nothing but a few scribbled lines in Christmas and birthday cards—it was Kim. Her voice was so familiar it had become a part of him, a part he both loved and hated. As the message ended, he took a couple of steps backward, staggering slightly, and sat down heavily on his bed. *"Hell."*

Jax had only harbored one great passion in his life—Kimberly Norman. As a kid he'd been a distracted geek, way too intense, oblivious to the subtleties of high school social politics. But Kim never seemed to notice his shortcomings. She'd been his friend, laughed at his dumb geek jokes.

She never seemed bored when they were together, even when he went on and on about circuitry or motherboards. She helped build more than one of his Science Fair projects, even though she never knew what he meant when he explained them to her. Or cared, for that matter. He always thought she was terribly cute that way.

He knew about her unsettled home life, so his company was doubtless the lesser of two evils. Even so, she seemed to genuinely like being around him. And he loved having her around. Kim, the freckle-faced day-brightener, girl-next-door. He didn't think she ever quite understood how lovely she was or how lucky he felt to be on the receiving end of her smiles.

As a youth he adored her quietly. Years passed, years when he hoped for more than a friendship. But after he was kindly—

but definitely—shut down following a few fledgling dates, he faced the fact that Kimberly needed him as a friend. She certainly didn't need him as a suitor. By the time she was seventeen she had plenty of those. Her carrot-red braids had become a flowing, sexy mane of auburn flame. And no matter how much she hated the sprinkling of freckles across her nose and cheeks, in truth they were a charming enrichment to her delicate features.

When she came to him after breakups with boyfriends, he soothed her, grateful for that part of her she gave to him. But having her near, knowing she cared—but not enough—not in the way a man wants a woman to care, wore on him. He'd grown into a man, and a man could only stand so much. Finally, he'd had all he could stomach of her rebounding off him.

That's why he left St. Louis. That's why he wrapped himself in his dot.com business. Then, after he sold that and became a consultant, he buried himself in his new enterprise. One day, he hoped to forget Kim, find some other woman who could fill the hole in his heart that he'd wanted her to fill.

Unfortunately, it hadn't happened.

Not yet.

He glared at the answering machine; the message light no longer blinked. "Why the *hell* couldn't you have been a telemarketer."

He ripped off his tie and threw it to the carpet. "Did it never occur to you that your little 'Jax Fix' pop-in might be a problem for me?" He started to unbutton his dress shirt, then stopped, ran both hands through his hair. Moments ago he was bored and weary. Now he blazed with a crazy mixture of bitterness and longing. What was he going to do? "I'll call her back," he thought aloud. "Tell her I'm going out of town—on business." He shoved himself up to stand and headed for the phone to check his caller ID for her phone number. "Better yet, I'm leaving the country, for—for a month."

He lifted the receiver, began to punch out the numbers. As he did, something strange happened. With each successive button he pushed, he slowed. By the last number, he had gone stock-still, his finger suspended above the number. "What's wrong with you, man?" he gritted out. "Punch it! Before she leaves!"

He winced at a sudden thought and checked the time she had made the call. Five-thirteen. He flicked a narrowed glance at his wristwatch. Ten-thirty-five. Reality lashed like a whip. Heaving an exhale as raw as a blasphemy, he lowered the phone to the ebony bedside table. If he knew Kimberly at all— and he knew her well—she was on her way.

The doorbell chimed, thundering in the quiet like a tractor-trailer truck barreling through his bedroom. He wheeled toward the sound, resentful, infuriated, yet on fire for her. *"Damn it, Kimberly!"* he ground out in a burst of frustration and rage. "I refuse to be your rebound man again. If you can't *be* my life, I want you out of it!"

He headed for the front door. With every step he repeated his manifesto to resist her.

Could he?

This time?

"Of course you can, you stupid *ass*."

Stark, lung-constricting, muscle-cramping doubt twisted his insides.

CHAPTER TWO

THE instant Jax opened his door she leapt at him. Womanly curves registered cruelly on every nerve ending her body touched. Arms encircled his neck and feathery kisses dampened and warmed his tensed jaw. He squeezed his eyes shut, in pain. This wasn't doing his vow to resist her any favors.

He inhaled, an unfortunate necessity, since her scent further degraded his declaration of resistance. He groaned inwardly, only half focusing on what she said between breezy kisses. With great reluctance, but undeniable desire, he enfolded her in his arms.

"Oh, Jax," she said in a long sigh, her sweet breath tickling his chin. "It's been too long."

She clung, gifted him with light, beguiling jaw kisses as she spoke. "I've missed you so much." She paused, smiled. Her green eyes glistened a bit too much, as though they were teary. Still, Jax found them to be the most breathtaking sight he'd seen in—well, for almost ever. At least since the last time he looked into them. His resistance crumbling, he smiled at her, hating himself but helpless against the depth of his feelings. "Hi, Kim." He hugged her, fighting the urge to cover those full lips with his, show her exactly what brand of greeting he ached to give her. If she knew the immensity of his restraint, she would blush as brilliant as her auburn hair, dazzling in the porch light. "It's—good to see you," he said against her temple, meaning it. Damn him.

"Oh, Jax!" she said, her voice sweet but melancholy. He knew exactly what that meant. Another man had broken her heart. He tensed. "I hope you don't mind my coming, but I really need you right now."

Yeah, he thought, *you need me right now. I need you every blasted minute of every blasted day.* Naturally he didn't say that aloud. Playing his part as the dutiful friend, he asked, "What's wrong?"

She loosened her grip on his shoulders and drew far enough away to look into his face. Her smile, though tentative and tremulous, blew him away. If he were a man who cried in the presence of great beauty, he would be in tears. "Oh, Jax..." she whispered again, then bit her lip, the expression sexy as hell, though he knew she had no inkling. "Could we go inside? I—I'd rather not..." She indicated his front porch. Wide and deep, it held a couple of padded chairs on either side of a small table. Late September in Chicago could be nippy, and she wore no coat. "...I mean, it's rather personal."

"Sure." *That's right, idiot. Do exactly what you swore you wouldn't do. Face it. You have no will of your own where Kim is concerned.* He released her and indicated her suitcase. "I'll take that."

Thanks." She preceded him into his three-story condo. "The flight of steps to the porch almost killed me, lugging that bag," she said.

"That's the downside of stacking a fourplex of condos on one narrow lot. It makes the first floor the garage." Kim grasped his hand as they came inside. He felt it too deeply and tugged free to wave toward the staircase, showing her the way to the bedroom floor. "I'll take your bag to the guest room. You'll probably want to freshen up."

She gazed around his luxury condo, the dark granite surround of the fireplace, the earth tones, from the mossy suede couch, rust-dyed drapes, the punches of gold and red in throw pillows and accessories, to the sleek chocolate-glazed accent tables. "You have a nice place." She faced him and smiled. "Fashionable, yet masculine."

He shrugged. "I bought it furnished."

She looked him up and down, then took his hand again. "Well, it's very put together." She squeezed his fingers affectionately. "So are you, by the way. I like the suit trousers and dress shirt. I'd call that look 'casual elegant.'" She grinned. "Did you get all casual elegant for me?"

He shook his head. "I just got home and was changing when I got your message. Another minute and I'd have been a little too casual and a lot less elegant."

She laughed. The musical lilt sent a sharp pain straight to his heart. "You mean you got my message minutes before I rang the doorbell?"

"'Fraid so."

She stuck out her lower lip in a pretend pout. "Then I'm disappointed. I thought you'd prettied up for me."

He frowned as he always had when she put on a pout. Once again he removed his fingers from hers. "I prettied up for a client dinner."

"Oh." She clasped her hands before her and nodded. "I see. Well, I guess I can get over the blow to my ego."

He scanned her from head to toe, admitting only the smallest fraction of what he thought. "You don't look so bad yourself." Raising an eyebrow at her, he asked, "I presume you got all—" he wanted to say adorable, but thought better of it "—chic for me."

She touched the collar of her pink linen suit jacket. "This thing? I flew from Vegas to St. Louis earlier today. Then when—" She cut herself off, swallowed. "Anyway, then I flew here. If I'm not a wrinkled, grimy mess, it's a miracle."

To him she looked like she'd stepped out of a fashion magazine. "Since neither of us prettied up for each other, and our egos are sufficiently crushed, do you want to freshen up or talk first?"

She seemed to give the matter a moment's thought. When her glance drifted to the staircase, he knew her choice before she spoke. "I think I'd like to take a good soak and get into sweats." She looked at him, her expression one of hope. "Will you still be up?"

What could he say? He wanted to be asleep. He should be asleep. It had been a very long day. But he knew even if he blew her off and went to bed, he'd get no sleep tonight. Not with her in the next room. "Since when have I not been here for you when you wanted to talk?" he said. *Why are you going to be here for her now? Are you that much of a glutton for punishment?* he admonished inwardly, but he wasn't listening to reason. He was too focused on Kimberly's beautiful eyes.

"I'd have to say you've always been there for me." She smiled, reaching up to pat his cheek. "I'll be down in a half hour."

"Would you like something to eat."

"I'd kill for some of your great pancakes."

"Pancakes, it is." He carried her bag up the steps, watching her as she moved ahead of him. Her long, slim legs hypnotized him. The slight sway of her hips transfixed him. The swinging bounce of her hair tormented him. He bit back an oath. When they reached her room he set down her bag. "See you...whenever," he said, feeling uncharacteristically awkward.

"See ya, Jax." She hugged his neck and planted a kiss almost—but not quite—on his lips. She and her suitcase had disappeared before he could breathe again.

When he managed to turn away from her door, he ground out, "*Blast you,* Jax." He headed downstairs. "You are the world's heavyweight champion fool."

Kim lounged in a tub of steamy water, her hair piled in a swirly heap on top of her head. Bubbly jets massaged her from all sides. Such luxury. Jax had come a long way since the days when he lived in the cookie-cutter tract house next door. She loved this bathroom. All marble and mirrors, and the guest room closet was huge. Empty and huge. Well, it was empty before she hung up her stuff. She sighed and inhaled the fragrant air. She could smell Jax's cologne. Odd. Maybe it was in her hair. She reached up and tugged down a strand and sniffed. "Ah," she said through a sigh. His scent lingered there. "You smell so good." She inhaled deeply once more before stuffing the strand back up out of her face.

She closed her eyes and thought about him. How great he looked. Had she ever seen him in a suit before? She couldn't recall. Though he didn't have on a tie or suit jacket, he still looked very dashing, very *GQ*. And she liked his hair. She'd forgotten how shiny and soft and jet-black it was. With just a touch of curl. When it was slightly mussed, and an errant lock fell across his forehead, he gave off appealing, swashbuckling-pirate vibes. For a science geek, it was totally against type, but charming. His hair had been that way tonight. Slightly disheveled with a hint of "rogue pirate." While the rest of his attire spoke of solidness, reliability and good character, that one curl screamed "sexy bad boy."

She giggled at the absurd notion. The preoccupied nerd who won Science Fairs, who was valedictorian of his senior class and whose dog never ate his homework, a *bad boy*!

"Very funny," she said aloud. She'd purposely dropped the word "sexy" from the "bad boy" image, since long ago she'd placed Jax in a category where sexy and sex and all its ups and downs had no place.

Suddenly restless, she decided she'd soaked long enough. Besides she could smell pancakes. She turned off the stimulating jets and rose from the tub, feeling better, at least physically. The delicious aroma of the pancakes reminded her she hadn't eaten since breakfast, a cold muffin and bitter airport coffee as she ran for her flight.

"Jax," she said as she toweled off with the softest, thickest navy terry towel she'd ever seen, "You are my rock. I love you." She grimaced, stopped, then shrugged it off. "Of course you love him," she said. "He's your best friend in the world. You can say 'I love you' and not rock any boats." She hung her towel on its bar and walked into a bedroom decorated in tasteful shades of green and beige. "Naturally, though, you probably shouldn't say it to him."

She didn't know why not, really. It just seemed like going too far. Every man to whom she'd said those three words had eventually walked out of her life. "No," she said. "That must never happen to me and Jax."

A few moments later, dressed in comfortable navy sweats and a pair of thick athletic socks, she bounded down the stairs. "It smells good in here," she called. "Where are you, Jax?"

"In the Lunar Module preparing for landing. Where do you think?"

She laughed, amazed that she could. "In the Lunar Module preparing for landing, of course. I keep up." Around the corner from the main living area, she headed past a contemporary dining-room table and chairs. Beyond that she spied a door and walked through it into the kitchen where a small, round oak breakfast table and four matching chairs snuggled in an alcove before a floor-to-ceiling bay window.

Outside, Kim could see the light show of downtown Chicago's high-rises. When she turned away from the scenery, she noticed the table set for one, and looked curiously at Jax. Shirtsleeves rolled up to his elbows, he stood over a skillet. A platter sat beside the gas range piled high with pancakes. "Hey, how many of those do you think I can eat?"

He turned toward her. "You mean I can stop now?"

"You could have stopped about a dozen pancakes ago." She plunked her hands on her hips. "In case you haven't noticed, I'm attempting to keep my figure."

He turned away and flipped the last pancake on the griddle. "Can't say that I have," he murmured.

"Gee thanks." She took an extra minute to gaze at him. He was such a wonderful person, and he'd matured into a very handsome man. She couldn't recall his shoulders being that broad, or his hips that trim. "Do you work out?" she asked, then registered she'd said it aloud. She snapped her gaze from his buttocks to his face just as he turned to look at her.

"What?"

She shrugged sheepishly. "Making conversation. I asked if you work out."

"Oh." He nodded and turned away. "I hit the gym several times a week."

"See, I can compliment you even if you can't compliment me," she teased. "You have a great butt."

He glanced at her again, this time frowning slightly. "Thanks."

She walked up behind him and slid her arms around his chest to hug him from behind. He felt solid. *My good, solid Jax.* She inhaled. *My good, solid, great smelling Jax.* "Isn't it weird the way we can be apart for so long, but we get back together and it seems like we just saw each other yesterday? I don't feel like I've been away at all."

He said nothing for a moment then, "Yeah." He sounded a little hoarse. After a few more seconds, he gently disengaged her hold on him. "Weird isn't the word." He turned off the gas and headed to the refrigerator. "Do you want butter, syrup, whipped cream or all of the above?"

Left alone facing the gas range, she made herself useful by taking the serving platter to the table. "Syrup and butter." She pulled out the chair where he'd set a plate and silverware, then paused to glance at him. "Do you have any nonfat butter?"

A corner of his mouth lifted, but less with mirth than cynicism. "Yeah, sure."

She shook her head. "Oh, fine. All my efforts will take a big nosedive if you feed me like I'm a two-hundred-fifty-pound trucker."

"Your reservations were relatively last minute. Even I need a little time to tend to details like nonfat butter, if there is such a thing."

"Okay, okay." She sat down. When he brought the syrup dispenser to the table she took his wrist. "Aren't you going to join me?"

"I just ate." He took an adjacent seat. His knee grazed hers but she didn't move away. When he did, she experienced a stab of deprivation. She couldn't quite put her finger on it, but Jax seemed somehow different. Like he wasn't completely thrilled that she was here. *Oh, that's crazy Kimberly,* she told herself. *He's your best friend and you're his. You're just super-sensitive right now.*

"I'm here to listen, remember?"

His prompt brought her back. She nodded. The reminder of why she'd come to him rushed back full force, almost overwhelming her. She struggled to keep from bursting into tears. She stared at the platter of pancakes for a time, then picked up her fork and stabbed several, sliding them onto her plate. She spread butter over them and doused it all with syrup. With a quick, grateful smile in his direction, she picked up her fork, cut into the stack and took a bite. Delicious. Jax's pancakes were so light and airy they melted in her mouth. She winked her approval at him, feeling less depressed. Upon finishing the first taste, she said, "You, Mr. Gideon, should be in jail."

"What?" His brow crinkled. He looked so cute she felt a zing in the pit of her stomach. "Why?" he asked.

"Because, it's a crime that you didn't go into the pancake-making business. That's why."

He lay a forearm on the table and leaned toward her. "I think you're stalling." His expression was gentle, earthy brown eyes direct. "So tell me. What happened to get you up here to doom me to prison in the middle of the night?"

"It isn't the middle of the night." He might be right. She probably was stalling. But she didn't intend to admit it, so she checked the kitchen wall clock and said, "It's not even midnight."

"Okay, so what got you up here at 'not even' midnight?"

She cut into the pancakes and took another bite. This time she had more trouble swallowing. Not because the food was any less delicious, but because Perry's desertion loomed so large in her mind. The harsh image of that empty condo and the pile of rejected gifts hurt to think about.

Her meal blurred and she blinked back tears. Realizing putting it off would make the telling no less hurtful, she laid her fork aside, but couldn't bring herself to look at Jax. "Okay, I thought I'd found Mr. Right. But when I got home from a business trip today, I found our place empty, except for a few shirts and other things I'd given him, in an insulting little lump on the bare floor." She rushed through the story, not wanting to prolong it with whimpery details. "He left a note. Called me commitment phobic and—and…" She choked back a sob. If she planned to make it through without crying, she'd better hurry. "And…well, his rejection was out of the blue—and his so-called reason for leaving totally *untrue*. Just because I didn't want to get married, doesn't mean I wasn't committed."

She stared blankly at her cooling food, forearms on the table, every ounce of her attention attuned to the man whose opinion she held in the highest regard. He said nothing for a long time. So long, in fact, she cast him a sidelong look. He was frowning—thoughtful? Compassionate? Dubious that her argument had a leg to stand on? She couldn't tell. "Gee, thanks, Jax. I'm all better now," she quipped with false enthusiasm, hoping to prod him into revealing what hid behind that frown.

"He took your things, too?" he asked.

"My things?"

He nodded. "Your furniture, rugs, whatever."

"Oh." Why did he have to zero in on that one tiny inconsistency for her "commitment" argument. "Does my heart count?" she asked, wanting to impress upon him what was important here and what wasn't.

She got a reaction. He winced a little. "Sure, it matters. I meant did he steal your things?"

"No, nothing like that. He left my clothes, the two framed prints I'd bought and a what-not shelf I took from my room when I left home."

"That's all that was yours?"

She didn't like the direction this conversation was taking. "So what? What are *things*? It's the emotions of a relationship that matter, and my emotions were *totally*—committed." Why did she falter on that last word? She *had* been committed to Perry and to their future together.

"Hmmm." He nodded, his expression solemn. "But you didn't want to get married?"

"What are you, a prosecuting attorney?" she asked, trying to keep things light so that his probing wouldn't bug her. She didn't want to be mad at Jax. "It's not a felony to say *no* to a marriage proposal."

He didn't smile.

"Come on, Jax. Lighten up. My heart may be broken but I don't need a transplant. Just tell me it'll be okay and give me a hug and help me heal like always."

He cocked his head, watching her. "So you came here for a hug?"

She broke eye contact, embarrassed and unsure why. Antsy, she picked up her fork and toyed with it. "Well…*duh.*" She ran the fork prongs through the melted butter and syrup, making a curvy row of lines from one edge of the plate to the other. When she peeked at him again, she was serious. "You know my mother's story, Jax. Marriage doesn't guarantee anything. I thought we were fine the way we were. Why rock the boat with meaningless contracts and promises?"

"Apparently they weren't meaningless to him."

She hadn't come here for an inquisition. "Since when did you join the debate team?" she asked, annoyed. "I need a friend—a hug—not a cross-examination." Slapping her palms to the table, she bolted up. "Look, if you can't see that he was in the wrong, then I made a mistake coming to you. I thought you were my friend."

"I am your friend. I'm only trying to get the whole picture."

"The whole picture is I'm upset and I need you to be on my side. Be my friend. Tell me he's a beast and I'm well rid of him."

"Okay, he's a beast and you're well rid of him," he dead-panned.

She crossed her arms and glared. "That's a good start. Now let's work on making it sound like you mean it."

He eyed her silently, then said, "I am your friend, Kim. But a friend tells you the truth. If you want a yes-man then you'll have to hire one. From me, you get honesty."

"Is that so?" she asked, "Then how much would you charge to be my yes-man?"

"Stop kidding."

"I'm not kidding." She struggled to keep from bursting into tears. She didn't know why she was so agitated or why she was on her feet. Apparently her relaxing bath with all those yummy bubbly jets were no match for Jax's disapproval, even if, at this stage, it was only a possibility on the horizon. She patted around on her hips as though searching for pockets. "I don't have any money on me, but if I run upstairs and get ten bucks, would it buy me a 'Perry is a big jerk and everything will be all right'?"

"Perry."

"Huh?"

He seemed to have turned inward for a second. When she spoke, he refocused on her. "Nothing." Appearing vaguely troubled, he worked his jaw. She wondered what he was thinking. After a second, he indicated her food. "Why don't you eat, then get a good night's rest. We can talk when you're fresher." He stood. "I think it would be best if I leave you alone for a while."

She was so surprised and disconcerted by his abrupt decision to go, she couldn't move or speak. She didn't want him to leave. The whole point of coming here was to be with him. When she opened her mouth to say so, he stopped her by taking her arm and firmly guiding her back to the chair. "Sit." With both hands on her shoulders, he coaxed her down. "Eat."

Once sitting, she stared up at him. "But—"

"You're tired. I'm tired," he said, before she could go on. "I can see you're in no mood to be rational."

"Rational!" She started to stand, but he foiled her plan by placing a restraining hand on her shoulder.

"Sit." He shook his head at her. "Stay."

She made a face. "I am *not* your dog."

He exhaled heavily and turned away, mumbling something that sounded like "A dog would be less trouble and more affectionate."

"What?"

He didn't turn back, merely shook his head. "I said leave the dishes and turn off the lights as you go to bed."

"That's not what it sounded like."

"Good night, Kim," he called back, disappearing from view.

She glared at the empty kitchen door, fists balled. After a few seconds, she calmed down enough to realize he was right. She needed time and distance from this afternoon to be totally rational on the subject of Perry's desertion. Jax was an expert on "totally rational" because if there was one thing Jax was, besides brilliant, it was rational.

She could hear his rapid tread as he jogged up the stairs two at a time. He was really going. "Hey," she shouted. "What happened to my hug?"

Somewhere in the distance a door slammed.

CHAPTER THREE

FOR Jax the night became an endless roller-coaster ride. He got no rest, tossing, turning, pacing and glaring out of the window, then tossing and turning some more. He couldn't bear to have Kim around, so near him, her scent driving him to distraction, her soft, radiant hair begging to be stroked. Her blasted need to be hugged, with those "best friend" pecks on his cheeks and jaw driving him crazy. Was it possible she didn't know what she did to him? Or was she so narcissistic she needed to torture him to get her jollies?

He ground out a blasphemy. Of course, she didn't know. He blamed his frustration and fatigue for such asinine thinking. Standing before his window, exhausted yet wide-awake, he peered at his watch. Illuminated by the rosy glow of dawn, its silver hands broke the bad news: 5:33 Heaving a weary groan, he decided he might as well go in to work. Yawning between mumbled curses, he went through the motions, his mind clouded by conflicted emotions.

He heard no stirrings from the guest room, so he quietly went downstairs to find the kitchen spotless. Apparently Kim hadn't left the dishes after all. "Thanks for that, at least," he grumbled. "You kept me up all night, wanting you, knowing I can never have you, but the dishes are clean."

Resentment spiked in him. The trade-off was light-years away from being even.

By rote he made his usual pot of coffee and filled his insulated travel mug. Before he left he scribbled Kim a note about being back around six, suggesting she relax and promising to bring home the makings for her favorite dinner. Taco salad. A favored meal would set a better tone for a frank discussion. Perhaps she might even be willing to admit her commitment phobia. Maybe she could begin to understand that if she ever wanted to have a lasting relationship with a man, she needed to deal with that first. If he did his job as friend and fixer well, one day Kim would find lasting happiness with some man.

Some *other* damn man.

He headed down the stairs to his garage, slid into his Jaguar coupe, and fired up the engine. "The irony is," he muttered, "the one relationship she's genuinely committed to is ours—so pathetically platonic it's killing me."

At six-thirty, he arrived at the high-rise office of Gideon and Ross, Business Productivity Consultants, to find his partner, Tracy Ross, already there. No great shock, since she practically lived in her office. Her door stood open, so as he passed by he crossed her line of sight.

"Hey," she called, "I didn't expect you for another hour. What gives? Problem?"

He didn't want to air his "problem" with Tracy, but knowing her burr-under-the-saddle personality, he might as well come clean, or she'd poke at it until it bled. Tracy was an exceptional businesswoman and an able partner, but she was an equally exceptional snoop with an exceptional snoop's radar.

He glowered at her. "Is it illegal to come in early?"

She grinned at him from behind her polished steel and Plexiglas desk. Tracy was a handsome woman with a close-cropped cap of naturally platinum hair and features made striking by exquisite bone structure. Designer half glasses perched on her slender nose. In heels she towered nearly as tall as he, which made her an intimidating six-three. She was as no-nonsense in business as she was classy in her choice of attire. Without any long-term, personal relationships and no interest whatsoever in the male sex, her life was her work.

Therefore, their business relationship was simply that, uncomplicated by sexuality. They both knew that many of their clients assumed they were lovers. The premise amused them. In actuality, they were a well-oiled machine, moving up fast in their profession, with an outstanding reputation for competence and positive results. He respected Tracy, prized her business acumen, was comfortable with their relationship, except at moments like these, when a male partner would ignore an awareness of a problem or never detect one at all.

"It's not illegal to come in early, Jax Man." She removed her reading glasses and set them on the legal-size notepad in front of her. "If it were, I'd be a lifer." She motioned for him to come in. "I brought muffins."

He half smiled. Even as all-business as she was, there were times when she reminded him of his grandmother. "Homemade?"

"Naturally." She shoved the open tin toward him. "These are not only delicious, they'll add ten years to your lifespan." As he approached her desk her grin faded. "Man, you look like twenty miles of bad road."

Here it came. "Only twenty?" he asked, his tone sardonic.

"I was being generous. It's more like fifty."

"Ah, the truth," he said, without smiling. "Doesn't that feel better?"

"I'll have to get back to you on that." She lifted the tin in his direction, as though it was imperative that he benefit from their life-enhancing sustenance. "I bet you haven't eaten."

"Wrong." He lifted his insulated mug.

She wrinkled her nose. To her, caffeine was poison. "You need a muffin. Did you even shave?"

He thought he had but he felt his jaw to verify. Instead of smooth skin he detected definite stubble. "Damn. I guess not."

She set down the tin. "I've never seen you with a 6:30 a.m. shadow before." Pausing, she assessed his new look, then shook her head. "I have to say, on a scale of one to ten, with ten being fantabulous, I give it a minus one thousand."

"Oh?" He raised an eyebrow at her barbed assessment. "When you make up your mind about how you really feel, don't hesitate to tell me." He picked up a muffin and took a bite. For health-nut food, it was actually good.

"So what brings you here at daybreak with us workaholics? Or are you coming down off an all-night bender? Maybe you spent the night in jail for speeding around in that British playtoy you drive?" She eyed him critically as he finished the muffin and downed the rest of his coffee. "On third thought, after I left you at dinner last night, did our client, Derk, drug your coffee and have his way with you in the alley?"

Jax didn't have to work hard to show aggravation. Frustrated and tired, he was in no mood for jokes. "A comedienne you're not."

She sat back in her jade-green leather chair and clamped her hands on the padded arms. "Okay, you tell me what brought you in here at this hour, looking like a hit-and-run victim?"

She didn't know how painfully close to the truth her comparison came. Characterizing Kim's connection to Jax as hit-and-run was horribly precise.

He propped a hip on the corner of Tracy's desk, and broke eye contact to gaze unseeing out of the window. He glanced down at Lake Shore Drive. Bumper to bumper traffic snaked along as the morning rush hour kicked into gear. His gaze drifted across the greenbelt of parkland and trees to Lake Michigan, sparkling in the morning sun like a placid, inland ocean. "Kim's here," he said simply.

A silence filled the room that was so profound it had the effect of a shrill, protracted scream. Tracy remained uncharacteristically mute for a long time. Though their partnership started after he'd last seen Kim, Tracy knew about her—of her acceptance of him when others thought he was weird. Of her generosity, her warmth and her easy laughter that could brighten even the most awkward and alienated geek's gloom.

Tracy knew being with Kim was like being home, to Jax. She also knew, with every date Jax went on with another woman, he tried to wash a bit more of Kim's memory from his heart. Kim had been the warmth in his life, a warmth he still struggled to learn to live without.

"Oh," she finally said. Right now he wished he'd never told Tracy about Kim. Hearing pity in her voice made him cringe. After another drawn-out silence, she asked, "Why now? After all this time when you'd almost..." She didn't go on, but he knew what she meant. When he'd almost broken free of the hold she had over him.

He returned his attention to her face. She looked so sad for him he felt a tug of compassion and tried to shrug it off. "The usual. Another broken heart."

"And you're supposed to fix it," Tracy said.

He grinned with bitter irony. "When she says she needs her Jax Fix, she's usually talking about a heart overhaul."

"Lord!" Tracy bent over and bumped her head on the legal pad, a prime theatrical bit. With her face on her desk, she covered the top of her head with her hands. "Now that I've heard everything, I might as well croak."

He looked out of the window again, then back at his partner, so dramatically overwhelmed. "It's what she needs," he said quietly.

Tracy rolled to her cheek and frowned at him from her desktop-view. "What about your needs, Jax?" She sat up and lay her hands flat on the desk. "You've told me enough that I know it kills you to be with her, yet—not be…"

He appreciated her loyalty and sensitivity and reached over the muffin tin to lay his hand across hers. "You're a good friend, Trace. And it is hard, but…" How did he put into words the horror that squeezed his heart at the thought of never seeing her again. Being with her was hell, but all the years he'd been without her had been worse. At a loss, he shrugged. "It's complicated."

Tracy snorted. "If I had one measly dollar for every time I've heard that pruney old cliché from a friend in a one-sided relationship, my household staff would consist of *France*."

He squeezed her fingers and kidded, "Instead you can only afford to employ the population of little old Nebraska."

She smirked. "Okay, laugh it off. But clearly the matter of our success doesn't solve life's problems because you—who could actually afford to employ all of France—look like you just clocked off a gritty, all-night shift in hell."

He stood up. "Then I'd better go shave."

"That would be a start, since looking the way you do, you'd scare the hirelings." She flicked her wrist over to check her gold watch. "Speaking of whom, a few early birds will be arriving very soon."

He nodded. "Point taken."

As he walked away, she said, "I worry that she's using you."

"Don't worry about me, Trace." He left her office and headed toward his.

More than anything in the world, he wished Tracy's impassioned misconception of Kim were true. If she really were that selfish, using him to salve her ego, he could make quick work of ridding himself of her. But she wasn't, and deep down Tracy knew it. She knew Jax well enough to know he didn't suffer fools or false friends easily.

Kim was one of the most giving people he'd ever known. She simply took their closeness for granted, like breathing. If anybody deserved to be blamed, he did. It wasn't Kim's fault that he didn't have the guts or the heart to tell her how much her visits hurt. Being highly sensitive she would be wounded beyond repair to discover that the faintest touch of her hand could bloody his heart.

Kim heard the garage door open and knew Jax was back. That morning she was disappointed to find him gone. She'd hoped they could chat over breakfast. Last night she spent a lot of pent up energy going through his cabinets, planning a breakfast of veggie omelets, whole wheat muffins and her famous strawberry-banana smoothies. Hopefully tomorrow she could coax him to stay later, let her fix him breakfast, since he obviously consumed nothing this morning but coffee. She knew he had a busy life and she didn't want to impose. Just because she had a little free time and a broken heart was no excuse.

But he was home now and she planned to make herself useful. He was wonderful to let her show up out of the blue, so she wanted to make her time there as pleasant for him as she could. Tonight they'd have taco salads a la Kim. She checked herself in the mirror over the dining room buffet then fluffed her hair and the neck ruffle of her silk blouse. She was almost as excited to see Jax as she had been to see Perry. For different reasons, of course. Jax wasn't her lover. He was more important than a lover. He was, well, Jax.

She could hear footfalls on the back stairs that led up from his garage. When he came into the kitchen, she positioned her-self in front of the kitchen table, arms wide. "Well, give, Jaxon! I'm starved. Lets get going on those taco salads."

He carried a brown bag in each arm. "It's good to see you, too," he said, his smile half-cast.

She plunked her fists on her hips. "Well, naturally it's good to see you. That goes without saying. I always adore seeing you." She took one of the bags from his arms and gave him a smooch on the jaw. "Mmm, you smell good. What is that cologne?"

He walked to the stainless steel countertop and set down the other bag. "I think it's called Badboy."

She set her sack next to his. "Badboy?" Hadn't she used that exact description while thinking about him last night? She noticed the wayward curl that gave him such a roguish qual-ity dangling over his forehead. "'Badboy is very appropriate."

He'd begun to empty the groceries. When she made the re-mark he paused, glanced at her. "It is?"

She laughed at his dubious tone. Clearly he'd never thought of himself as a bad boy. She reached up and ran a finger along the errant lock. "That's the bad boy look I love, right there. Such a deliciously delinquent curl. It makes you seem so…" She stopped, thought about it. "So…" The word "sexy" al-most slipped out but she caught it in time and searched for a substitute word.

"So—what?"

Feeling oddly restless she lowered her hand from his hair and looked away, busying herself with the groceries. "Oh, uh, I don't know. Like a mobster or something."

"A mobster?" He sounded doubtful. "A la Al Capone?"

She couldn't help smiling and glanced his way. "Well, maybe a mobster's accountant."

He squinted at her, evidently not flattered by the compar-ison. Could she blame him? But she dared not admit that the misbehaving curl made him look like a sexy pirate. Such a remark would be blatant flirting, and—well, that's not why she came to Jax.

He raked his fingers through his hair. "If we're through discussing my hair, why don't you finish putting this stuff away while I change."

"Sure." She avoided eye contact. "Take your time. Even better, let me fix the salads. You relax. You've had a long day."

"No, I said I'd help. I'll be right down."

"Don't be silly."

He stilled. She couldn't help looking at him and experienced a tingle of pleasure at the sight. His attempt at erasing the mobster curl had failed. "I have a secret ingredient," he said. "Therefore you can't do it alone."

She cocked her head in playful challenge. "Oh, really?"

He nodded, appearing serious. "Just grate the cheese. Is that understood, woman?"

Clamping her lips together she fought a grin. When she could manage it without giggling, she said, "My, how masterful you've become."

He indicated the cheddar on the counter. "Just grate. I'll be right back."

She elbowed him lightly in the ribs. "Don't let that mobster accountant thing go to your head."

He turned away, headed toward the door. "You can't unring a bell, sweetheart." His voice mimicked the distinctive delivery of an old-time movie tough guy.

"Heaven help me," she said, laughing. "I've created a monster."

"No, a mobster's accountant," he corrected in the same tough-guy voice.

After he disappeared from view, she took up the cheese package and began to open it, grinning to herself. Jax could be so cute. Strange. She had a perfectly awful day, accented by bouts of crying and feeling sorry for herself. Then Jax shows up, and—*bam!*—sunshine streams in to warm her cold, old soul.

After dinner, Kim insisted they leave the dishes for her to do later. She took Jax by the hand, leading him into the living room to drink their coffee. When they reached the sofa she gently pushed him down, then took a seat, kicked off her sneakers and curled up on the far side. "Can we have a fire?" she asked, feeling better than she had all day. "I love the smell."

"Sure." He grabbed a remote off the end table and pressed a button. Instantly fire flared in the hearth.

"Oh—my—heavens!" She giggled, set her coffee on the end table and leaned over to run a hand along his biceps. "What a pioneer type you are. That must have been quite a strain."

He lay the remote aside. "The wood fairy didn't carry in that wood, you know."

She smiled. "I'm kidding. Your place is awesome. Push-button fires, yet." She lounged back, picked up her coffee, but continued to look at him. He'd changed into jeans and a soft, golden sweater that accented his torso nicely. Looking at Jax made her feel better, and she sighed. Then she had an amusing thought. "So your secret taco ingredient is taco seasoning, huh?"

He peered her way. "Yep."

She laughed. "I hate to tell you, but your secret's out."

He frowned, faking shock. "No."

She nodded, giving him a pitying look. "'It's true."

"Damn. There goes my shot at a show on the cooking channel."

She laughed, scanned his wayward bad boy lock of hair, his well toned chest, flat belly, solid thighs..."You work out, don't you?" she said, surprised to hear the remark aloud.

He sat his coffee on the sleek, espresso-brown coffee table. "I told you that last night."

How embarrassing. Not only because she had asked a second time, but because neither time had she meant to say anything out loud. She crossed her arms before her, pretending to be casual and conversational. "Oh? Must have slipped my mind," she lied. "Well, it shows." She winced inwardly. Had she lost the ability to think something without blurting it out?

His brow crinkled, as though he wasn't sure how to take the remark. "Thanks."

"Feel free to smile, Jax. I won't tell."

That remark provoked a bona fide glower.

She sat up, concerned, and scooted over to him. "What's the matter? Have I done something to upset you?" She took his hand. "I know I'm a terrible disruption, and I was only thinking of myself when I burst in on you. All through dinner all I did was babble about Perry and my job. It's been me, me, me, and you've been so good, listening and..." The sentence died as she had a distressing thought. "Heavens—it's a woman, isn't it?"

"What?" She'd clearly caught him off guard with that question. He stared, looking cautious.

"You have a girlfriend, and you think you have to neglect her while you baby me." She grasped his hand with both of hers. "That's it, isn't it? Well, you don't have to. I'd love to meet her," she said. "I don't want to screw up your social life. But that's exactly what I'm doing. You want to be with her and you have to babysit me." She felt terrible guilt. "I'm such a selfish—"

"No," he interrupted gruffly. "You're not a selfish anything. And there's no other woman I'd rather…" He paused, cleared his throat. "I have no one serious in my life at the moment, so don't beat yourself up for no reason. You know me well enough to know if I didn't want you around I'd…" He paused, looked as though he had a troubling thought.

"You'd tell me?" she prompted.

He glanced at his coffee cup, picked it up and took a gulp, then set it down heavily. "Yeah—right." After a second, he returned his attention to her face.

She showed her doubt by narrowing her eyes. "I don't know that I do know that, Jax. I can't remember you ever telling me to get lost as a kid. And I must have been an awful annoyance at times. A twelve-year-old kid tagging after a fifteen-year-old teenager." She cuddled up to him, hugging his arm with both of hers. "You never, ever told me to get lost. How could I know you'd tell me to now?"

"I never told you to get lost?"

She smiled. "Never. I would remember because I'd have been crushed."

He shifted his gaze to the fire. "Apparently I have a high tolerance for awful annoyances."

"So you're okay with me being here?"

He watched the fire without speaking.

"Jax?" she coaxed. "Did you hear me? Are you okay with me being here?"

"Sure," he said quietly. He glanced at her and nodded, his smile brief but as welcome as the fire's warmth. "Of course."

"I'm glad." She lay her head on his shoulder and closed her eyes. "Doesn't the fire smell nice?"

He didn't respond. At least Kim wasn't aware of any response. She was exhausted from the emotionally draining day. Stress had taken a toll, sapped her, and Jax's nearness felt so comforting. When sleep beckoned, she floated toward it, entirely relaxed for the first time in...too tired...to think...

Jax sat motionless, almost not breathing. Kim's scent coiled around him like a siren with no regard for the mortal soul damned to eternal loneliness by her flagrant yet innocent cruelty. Her breasts, pressed against his arm, burned seductively. His gut clenched with hot desire.

Steeling himself, he glared unseeing into the fire, its mellow, woody smell a poor second to the sweet essence of the woman cuddled there, unknowingly laying waste to his heart. After a mercifully short time, he could tell she slept by the low, even rhythm of her breathing.

To keep from waking her, he carefully disengaged himself from her grasp and lowered her head to a pillow. He covered her with a cashmere throw and turned off the table lamp. For a moment he couldn't move, so captivated by the sight of flickering firelight setting her hair aglow. A glossy tendril fell across her cheek. With no capacity or desire to resist, he smoothed it away from her face, then kissed the freckled cheek where the curl had rested.

She stirred, sighed, the slight, throaty sound piercing his heart. Abruptly he straightened and grabbed his cup, then retrieved hers. He had two choices, either clean up the kitchen or ravage the woman he wanted desperately *not* to love. Gritting his teeth on a curse, he distanced himself from her before he did something unforgivably stupid.

CHAPTER FOUR

THE next morning at the office, Tracy made it clear that Jax had seen better days. She was right. He hadn't slept much last night, either. And as was Tracy's way, she dragged every bit of information out of him that he was willing to share. The part about the kiss and his urge to debauch a defenseless, sleeping woman remained his guilty secret.

"So Kim's a professional meeting planner, you say?" Tracy asked, drawing him back from his reverie.

In Jax's office, where they often ate, the pair lunched on veggie subs, at Tracy-the-health-nut's insistence. She didn't consider lunchtime off-limits for strategy planning meetings. At least his office made these business lunches endurable, due to their bird's-eye view of Lake Michigan.

"Yes, she's a meeting planner," he said.

"That could work for us." Tracy sipped her herb tea.

He didn't understand. "What could work for us?"

"I'm saying we could put your troubling little houseguest to work. Have her be the official hostess for the Japanese CEOs coming to your country place."

Jax didn't like the sound of this, and shook his head. "I don't think—"

"You don't have to think, Jax Man, because since you

mentioned it this morning, I've done all the thinking that's necessary on the subject." She laid aside the last bit of her sandwich. "I've been stewing about this meeting ever since we decided to do it, and I believe Kim fell right into your lap at the perfect time."

"Stewing?" That wasn't a word he associated with his take-no-prisoners partner. "What have you been stewing about? Why haven't I heard about it?"

"Well..." She looked uncharacteristically embarrassed. "It probably seems petty to you, but remember that function last summer when we met with business owners from around the country?"

He nodded. "Sure."

"Do you remember my complaining about how several of them handed me coats and snapped their fingers at me when they wanted coffee refills. Remember how questions were directed to you and how I was pretty much ignored?"

He frowned. "I think you must be exaggerating."

"Not really." She shook her head adamantly. "I'd say a good third of them treated me more like a waitress, a coat-check girl, a secretary, even once a freakin' babysitter—and you know how I feel about kids—than your partner." She exhaled loudly, rolling her eyes. "I don't plan to let that happen again."

"The Japanese are a very progressive people. I'm sure—"

"You're probably right, but I'm not willing to take chances." She eyed him unblinking, her stare deadly. "Have you ever changed the diaper of a baby with the runs? It's no picnic, Jax. I don't intend to be thought of as anything this time but your partner. *Comprende?* Some cultures don't look at women the way ours does. They have more conservative notions about male vs. female roles and family values. Our Japanese guests may not have the slightest problem thinking of me, and treating me, as their equal. But at that thing last summer, with those good-old-boys snapping their fingers at me like I was a trained dog, well, it was humiliating, So even if there's only a one-percent chance I'd end up waitressing or holding coats next week, it's too chancy for me to cope with. I've been so worried I'll be relegated to hostess status, it's giving me an ulcer." She banged the table with a fist. "*Damn it, Jax,* I'm not a waitress or a coat-check girl or a babysitter, and I don't want those businessmen to assume I'm there for no other reason than to babysit their wives."

She paused, grim-faced. "I do *not* intend to stand around serving tea and petit fours, talking about child rearing or husbands, neither of which I know squat about. Nor do I *care* to know anything. I will *not* babysit those wives. It's not in my job description." She sat back, lolled her head on the chairback as though spent. "There I've said it." She let out a long, weary exhale, then lifted her head to look him in the eye. "Do not tell me I'm being silly, because if you do, I'll—I'll…" She sat forward, aggressively. "I'll *quit.*"

Jax could hardly believe Tracy's emotional torrent. Poor woman. Obviously Tracy's summer experience hadn't been good. She was truly frightened of being minimized at their upcoming conclave of Japanese CEO's. He laid aside his sandwich and leaned across the corner of the table to touch her fisted hand. "I can't believe I was so preoccupied with work I didn't even notice."

She smiled wanly. "I was a little hurt that you didn't."

"Why didn't you say anything?"

With his reassuring touch, she visibly relaxed and placed her free hand on his . "You know me. Never admit fear or defeat."

He grinned. "Yeah, well, from now on make an exception if it involves our partnership. Understood? I'll have no more talk about quitting."

She frowned, as though ashamed about her hesitance to reveal her apprehension. "Okay—well, now that you know my deepest, darkest fear, my thinking is, if we get Kim involved, we can kill two birds with one stone. She can get her Jax Fix, mend her fitful little heart and she can also make some money representing the traditional female role of hostess. That will leave me free to act as the equal partner I am. Is that an excellent idea or is it an excellent idea?"

Jax's initial inclination was to say no, but with Tracy's extreme anxiety, what could he do? "It isn't as though the plan isn't good," he said, feeling his way. "Except—then Kim would be around that much longer."

"True." Tracy nodded. "But has she mentioned leaving anytime soon?"

Jax pursed his lips. Nothing Kim had done or said so far had the earmarks of an impending departure. "No," he admitted.

"How long does she usually stay for these Jax Fixes?"

He shifted his gaze to stare unseeing out of the window, the view of Lake Michigan blocked by Kim's face—the way she looked last night, asleep on his sofa. "A week—or two." He flinched. Having Kim around, looking the way she did in the firelight—seemingly pliant and willing, yet in reality, oblivious and unsubmissive—would be like enduring two weeks crawling over broken glass.

"That's perfect!" Tracy's enthusiasm pulled him back in time to see her smile. "She'll have almost a week to plan, which isn't much, I'll grant. But everything as far as food, location and accommodations is already taken care of. She'd really only have to be there to oversee things, watch after the spouses while we're in meetings. That would be child's play for a professional like your Kim." She clapped her hands. "She's made to order."

He drummed his fingers, agitated. With this new wrinkle—the possibility of keeping Kim around to utilize her expertise—the burden of anxiety had clearly been passed from Tracy's shoulders to his.

"Oh, don't shake your head!" Tracy said.

He flicked his gaze to her. Had he been shaking his head?

"Look," she added gently, understanding in her eyes. "I know it's hard for you to be near her, but if she's going to be around anyway, why not use her? She gets her fix, you get a meeting planner and I get to be the partner I deserve to be, not a coffee toting toadie."

Though his mood was far from happy, he couldn't help but grin at her imagery. "I'd like to see somebody treat you like a toadie."

"Yeah?" she said. "Well, the next man who does will lose a favorite body part."

Jax's grin faded as he tried to get his mind around the whole Kim problem. He knew she would stay as long as she felt she needed to, but that didn't mean he had to do all the giving. From the moment she arrived on his porch, he'd been frustrated and angry to find her back in his life, complicating things, shredding his peace of mind.

To balance the scales, maybe he could use her for a change. It wouldn't be the kind of "using" that would break hearts, only the kind that would exploit her expertise. If he couldn't have her as his life, he wanted her *out,* and that had to include shucking the title of "friend." When all was said and done, he would have to lay it out for her, painful as it might be.

But for Tracy, for the present, he would bite the bullet. During the next ten days he would continue to play the role of friend and confidant to Kim, no matter how deeply it cut.

He refocused on his partner, decision made. "Okay," he said. "For you, I'll ask Kim to be our official hostess. Feel better?"

Tracy stood, walked around to him, took his face between

her hands and kissed his forehead. "You, Jax Man, are a prince."

After she left, he sat for a long time feeling like hell. "I'm sorry, Kim," he muttered. "But your dear old Jax is about to use you—then lose you. It's time." He slumped back and closed his eyes. "You'll hate me but...*blast it,* as hard as it will be for me to say goodbye, dealing with your anger, even your hatred, will be easier than living my life tortured by this unbearable, celibate intimacy we share now."

Kim couldn't believe her ears. Had Jax actually asked for her help? "Are you kidding?" she said, excited. "You want me to hostess your business meeting?"

He stood there looking so serious, as though he actually thought his request might be an imposition. "I would—that is my business partner and I would appreciate it."

She hugged him. "I'd be thrilled. You've done so much for me to let me come here and stay with you. And since I've got some free time before my next job, it would be my pleasure, my honor!" She slid her hands down his arms to affectionately squeeze his fingers. "This is right up my alley." She had a thought. "So what needs to be done? Set up catering? Arrange outings for the wives? Tell me and it's done."

He seemed thoughtful, his forehead crinkling. "Meals and housing and all that is set, but I hadn't thought of outings. That might be nice. Take the women..." He paused, as though without a clue about where they might go.

She laughed. "Leave that to me. No catering?"

"My housekeeper has arranged all meals, and the meetings will be at my country home, too, where they'll be staying," he said. "Basically, I need—a hostess."

She squeezed his fingers once more for emphasis. "Well, you've got yourself one."

"Thanks." He looked no more pleased than if she'd told him to go soak his head.

She released his hands. "Is this meeting what's been worrying you?" she asked. "I know you're not daunted by much, so what makes this gathering so important?"

"Tracy and I want to expand overseas."

"Ah." She understood. "It's a chance to grow the business."

"Yes, and Tracy pointed out she's had bad experiences in the past with more conservative businessmen about the roles of males and females. It's left a bad taste in her mouth. There may not be a traditionalist in the group, but on the chance there is, she's afraid she'd be reduced to a menial role, rather than—"

"No need to explain," Kim interrupted. "I'll play the part of menial hostess." She echoed his remark kiddingly, since she didn't see the role of hostess that way at all.

"I'm sorry. I didn't mean to suggest—"

"Shut up, Jax." She grinned, then something niggling in a corner of her brain needed to be voiced. "I didn't realize your partner was a woman."

"Didn't I mention that?" he asked.

She shook her head. "Not that I recall." This was an interesting development. A woman partner. A thousand scenarios popped into her head, but she shoved them aside. She had work to do, and only a few days to pull together a schedule of activities. "How many couples did you say would be coming?"

"Five."

"Do they all speak English or do I need to get an interpreter?"

"I believe they're fluent in English."

"Give me a list of their names and phone numbers. I'll check into it." This was exactly what she needed to take her mind off Perry, not to mention the perfect way to pay Jax back for all his kindness. She felt better than she had in—well, since she walked into her bare apartment.

"Of course, I'll pay you," he said.

She took his arm and walked with him into the kitchen, the scent of the roast beef she'd cooked for dinner wafting around them. "Hey, you try to pay me anything and I'll kick your shins." She elbowed him playfully in the ribs. "You know I will."

She peered up at him, watched his eyebrows dip at the recollection of the painful kicks she'd inflicted on him when, as a kid, he'd made her mad.

"I still carry the scars," he said, straight-faced.

She fought a smirk and held out a foot to show off a pointy-toed pump. "You only *think* scars. Try getting jabbed with one of these babies."

He eyed the stylish shoe. "Okay, since you put it that way, I won't pay you one red cent. Satisfied?"

"I'm glad we understand each other." She indicated the cabinet housing his china. "Set the table. Dinner's done."

"Bully," he kidded, more like his old self.

"Bad boy."

He halted, turned toward her. She reached up and swept the darling, errant curl off his forehead. "So *bad*," she said to the curl.

He looked up as though trying to catch a peek at the misbehaving lock of hair. "You seem to have a problem with my hair."

She wondered at the slight edge to his voice. "Don't be silly. It's the epitome of artful dishevelment, and quite se—*cute*." She'd almost said sexy! *Watch it, Kimberly. Those thoughts are allowed out for a temporary airing during solitary bubble baths. They are not to be poured out of your mouth in front of Jax.*

His lips tightened; his jaw flexed. "Whatever." Once again, her compliment seemed to be more aggravating than pleasing. She wondered what she'd done to upset him. "Jax, are you mad at me?"

"Why would I be mad?" he asked with maddening politeness.

She drew an uneven breath. "I don't know. You just seem—annoyed with me."

"How could I be annoyed with you?" He ran a hand through his hair, dislocating the brazen curl which tumbled across his brow once more, the sight too erotic for her peace of mind.

"That's what I'm asking you." Her temper flared at his continued vagueness. "Am I that much of a bother? If I am, Jax, tell me, please. The last thing I want is to be an imposition. You're my...my best friend," she said, her voice fragile. "I love you." Oh, she said it aloud! The shock of it lasted only a second, for she realized there was no harm in telling him. Surely he knew she loved him—in a purely platonic, best friend way.

He stood there, stock still, studying her for a long moment, his brown eyes direct and a little weary. "I know how you feel about me," he said, without inflection. Shifting away, he walked to the sink and began washing his hands. "I love you, too."

The way he said it—toneless, without joy—cut to the heart, as though he carried a burden, and that burden was his connection with her. "You say it like it's a bad thing."

He shrugged, his demeanor that of a man deliberately removing himself from a situation that was an obvious chore. She didn't want to believe his body language. Jax couldn't want to separate himself from their friendship. It had to be something else. Something simple, like a headache making him grouchy.

Whatever it was, she needed to get to the bottom of it. Moving up behind him, she hugged him around the waist and pressed her cheek against his back. She could hear his heart beating, strong, steady, like him. She inhaled his scent with great relish. "What can I do to make it better?" she asked. For an instant, when she first slid her arms around him, he went still, but quickly enough resumed soaping his hands. She felt the muscles in his back bunch and shift as he washed, then dried, his hands. "I want you to be happy, Jax. I want to see you smile, hear you laugh—like you used to."

"Chalk it up to jitters—about next week." He moved aside, out of her embrace, and headed for the cabinet with the dishes. "Leave it at that. Okay?"

Kim watched him remove two plates. After a second she realized her arms were outstretched, as though she still hugged Jax's waist. She dropped them. "That's new, isn't it?" Unable to think of anything else to do, she went about getting the pot roast from the oven.

"What?"

"Jitters," she said, dissatisfied with that explanation. "I don't remember you as a nervous type."

"People change."

"I suppose. But not into complete *other* people." She lifted the roast from the oven and set it on top of the stove, staring at it, unwilling to take his explanation at face value. "You've always been self-assured. I've never known you to fail at anything you tried." She glanced at him as he took down the plates. "Don't tell me you've changed that much. I find that difficult to swallow. Impossible, in fact."

He peered at her. "Maybe you should do my PR."

She smiled. "I'd be happy to."

He turned away.

She shook her head. It had to be a headache or something. She always used to be able to get him to smile.

Something nagged, then it came to her—that cryptic remark in Perry's note about never measuring up. Could Perry have been referring to Jax? Had her casual reminiscences about her lifelong friend have intimidated Perry?

Jax was good at many things, but she hadn't meant to demoralize Perry—or other men—with her references about his ability to do thus and so. Breezy remarks like, "Jax gave the best back rubs," or "Jax was a genius when it came to fixing my computer," or "Jax has a photographic memory." So what? Jax was her best friend. Why shouldn't she be proud of him and his accomplishments? Why not mention him in passing? She never meant to tear down Perry or other boyfriends who passed thorough her life with "Jax Facts."

And now Jax was telling her he was so nervous about next week's meeting he couldn't even crack a smile for his oldest, dearest friend in the world? It didn't make sense.

She heard the light tap of dishes being set on the kitchen table and looked over her shoulder to gaze at the man with the bad boy curl and such broad, capable shoulders. She experienced an odd buzzing in her chest. Strange. She'd felt the same sensation a time or two in the past few days when Jax came into a room. What was with her lately? It was almost like she was hot for the guy.

Hot for Jax? Her best buddy? Jax, the calm eye in the center of her life's hurricane? She watched him set the table, felt a tug of—something. What? She put the thought aside. Jax's friendship was too important to mess with. No rocking the boat where Jax was concerned. Without his friendship she would fall overboard and drown.

She scanned his profile. Had his lashes always been that long? His jaw that square? His belly that flat? Had he actually grown more handsome over the past decade? Probably not. It was her vulnerability right now. Seeing him again after being away for so long simply made him seem bigger than life. He was the same Jax. More serious, true, but otherwise, just the same.

She smiled at him, so masculine, so yummy, even doing a girly chore like setting a table.

Their glances caught and held. He paused, looked leery. "Something funny?" he asked.

She shook her head. "No. I was just looking at you." She turned away, knowing how lucky she was to have Jax for a friend. And with the hostessing job to keep her mind occupied—well, once again, Jax was the cure for what ailed her.

Just looking at him? Jax stared at Kim's back. The woman knew how to twist the knife. She *just* looked. *Just* smiled. *Just* hugged. She even just *kissed*—with absolute indiscrimination. And her careless "I love you" ambush clawed at his heart, leaving such raw, jagged gashes he could barely keep from screaming with the pain.

Sure, she thought she knew how he felt, or she knew as much as she could face knowing and "rock no emotional boats," as she put it. The truth would definitely rock boats. More like capsize them. He'd never been more conflicted in his life. He wanted to rock her boat, flip it over, sink the damn thing. But, deliberately hurt Kim? Frighten her with the knowledge that he loved her, not as a friend, but as a man? A red-blooded, mortal man, drowning in an endless, stormy sea of loneliness.

The truth would free him, for she would run. Because to Kim, intimacy between a man and a woman had to be free of conflict, because conflict lead to partings. She had never seen a healthy relationship working—couldn't imagine fighting, resolving problems, then going on together. No, he could never be her lover, her husband, because the moment they fought, she would end it. The inevitability of his life was to be cast out of hers.

If it weren't for the promise he'd made to Tracy, he would grab Kim, confess his love, declare that every moment spent near her, without the right to touch, was a moment in his own private hell.

Suddenly he could no longer cope with the idea of sitting down to dinner with her, could no longer deal with attempting polite conversation. His gut constricted with all the things he wanted to tell her, the charges he wanted to make about her faculty to be blind, closed up, unwilling to comprehend the truth about the men she thought she wanted, and most especially the one man she *thought* was her best friend—her rebound buddy—who, she assumed, would always be there to pick up the pieces. He was at the end of his rope with her blasted dependence on him as her Father Confessor.

To control his voice he counted to ten then replaced his plate on the shelf. "Look, Kim," he said, "I just remembered a business dinner. I've got to go." Without leaving her an opening, he headed toward the stairs to the garage. "I'll be back late. Sorry about dinner."

He bounded down the steps two at a time. For Tracy's sake, he hoped he could hold on to his self-control until Kim's hostess duties were done. Inside the garage, the door firmly closed behind him, he stopped, looked around dully, feeling like a burned out hulk. Where was he going? What was he doing? "Lord," he whispered, "when the times comes—help me get her out of my life—" his mouth was so dry he could hardly form the rest of his prayer"—and my heart."

CHAPTER FIVE

KIM felt good about the plans she'd made so far, and decided to get off the phone and out of the condo for the afternoon. Since she'd never seen Jax's office, she grabbed a cab, her plan to drop in for a quick tour. She missed him last night after he left so suddenly. He'd been gone before she stirred that morning, almost as though he was avoiding her. And why was he so serious?

She worried about that for much of the night, trying to figure it out. Finally, she concluded he had a toothache. He'd always been grouchiest when he had a toothache. Being a macho guy, he didn't even take an aspirin unless broken bones were involved, let alone call a dentist. Only when the pain was so bad he couldn't eat or sleep had he ever admitted his grouchiness was caused by excruciating pain. Yes, it had to be a toothache. Men! How silly they could be.

She laughed out loud, drawing the cabdriver's attention to his rearview mirror. Could it be that he didn't have many people burst into laughter for no reason? She smiled at the dark eyes peering suspiciously at her. "I adore riding in cabs," she said, feeling almost giddy for figuring out Jax's problem.

The swarthy driver grunted and returned his attention to the road.

When they arrived at the address, she hopped out and looked up at the gleaming steel and glass skyscraper. Like a giant mirror, it reflected sparkling Lake Michigan and a cloudless, azure sky. The Windy City had been blessed with beautiful weather on this waning September day, without a breath of its infamous wind. She smiled as she looked up at the building. "Oh, Jax," she said, "you shouldn't be grouchy on a beautiful day like this. I'm going to get you to that dentist because I miss your great smile."

Once inside, she scanned the list of building occupants, found Gideon and Ross Consultants and rode up the superfast elevator to the twenty-second floor. The elevator opened onto a reception area gleaming with smoked glass and ebony marble, stylized golden letters on the wall spelling out Gideon and Ross above an attractive blonde at the reception desk.

When Kim mentioned being Jax's houseguest, she was immediately directed toward his office. She felt quite important and lucky. Apparently being Jax's guest made her a VIP. It felt good after being dumped and rejected. Entering his outer office, she had a fun idea and asked his secretary if she could surprise him. The woman seemed about to reject the proposal when Kim interjected, "I'm his houseguest, from St. Louis. Kim Norman."

"Oh?" The woman upped her smile a notch. Once again, the magic of being Jax's intimate friend worked. "Of course, Miss Norman," the pretty brunette replied, her voice silky. Kim decided she probably sounded quite elegant on the phone. She certainly looked elegant. Altogether the perfect personal assistant. Leave it to Jax to gather perfection around him. "I'm sure Mr. Gideon would want you to go right in."

"Thanks." Kim breezed through Jax's door, a grin on her

lips and a "surprise" on the tip of her tongue. But before she could utter the word, she froze at what she saw.

Jax and a striking woman were chest to breast in what looked like an intimate encounter. They weren't quite kissing, but their lips were ominously close. The woman laughed. And Jax, *her Jax,* who had been so solemn for much of their visit, was chuckling—actually chuckling. The deep, rich sound bounced around painfully inside her skull. Apparently his toothache was better.

"Jax, you're tickling me." The woman clutched his shoulders, giggling, her lips a mere inch from his. "That's not playing fair."

"You're wiggling," he said, both hands at her breasts.

Her breasts!

"Because you're tickling!"

"Do you want me to do this?"

"Yes, *yes!*" she entreated, her voice husky and bubbly. "Please!"

"Don't wiggle, then."

"But I'm ticklish. You should know that by now."

"All over?"

"Stop with the twenty questions and just *do* it."

"I'm ripping it off."

"Yes! Rip it off!" She sounded eager. Or would a better word be aroused? "Jax, you're driving me mad!"

"Oh—*my...*" Kim blinked. Had she spoken aloud? Apparently so, because both Jax and the woman, who proved even more striking in the full-face view, looked her way.

"Kim?" His smile slipped, then disappeared as he drew away from the female. "I didn't..." He paused, flinched slightly, but said nothing more.

His partner in this lust-a-thon moved away, too, her expression amused. "Kim?" she asked. "So this is the childhood—

friend I've heard so much about." She glanced back at Jax, who wore a white dress shirt and tie. She patted him on his chest.

The familiarity of the gesture affected Kim like a physical blow. She felt dizzy and realized she was hyperventilating. She concentrated on slowing her breathing.

"Jax, honey—" the woman turned toward Kim "—thanks for the wrestling match." Her tone was matter-of-fact, as though she spent part of every afternoon being fondled—and heaven knew what else—in Jax's private office. Gathering up several files from the desk, the female clutched them to the same chest that so recently played willing hostess to Jax's hands. Apparently, there were *some* situations when Tracy didn't have a problem playing hostess.

Kim experienced a harsh chill slice through her body. She could only stare as the woman rounded his basketball-court-size desk and set a course directly for Kim. When she was a foot away, she held out a slender hand, clearly not a bit embarrassed she'd been caught with Jax's fingerprints all over her. "I'm Tracy Ross, Jax's partner. It's nice to put a face to the name."

Kim could hardly hear her, the blood pounded so hard in her ears. Though she had an urge to turn and run, she managed to remain outwardly calm. Years of training and reinforcement in the social niceties took over. She held out her hand and accepted the woman's. Tracy's hand was warm, which only told Kim that her own had gone icy. "How—do you do?" Dumb question. From what Kim witnessed, she obviously did fine. She tried not to shoot daggers through her eyes at the woman.

"Well, all play and no work," Tracy said with a brazen wink at Kim, "...is great fun, but it doesn't pay the bills." She released Kim's hand and turned to blow Jax an air kiss. "Thanks again, *snookums*." She headed for Jax's office door.

He watched her leave, his brow pinched, as though her cavalier chatter about their interlude didn't sit well with him. Kim could understand that. Jax had always been a private person.

Once Tracy was gone, Kim looked around dully, sick to her stomach. She couldn't fathom why she felt so lost. After all, Jax was a man, not a monk.

Gathering her poise, she faced at him, making a conscious effort to hold eye contact. His seductive good looks, and the memory of what just happened, were like a slap in the face. It stung. It shouldn't, but it did. With great effort she gave a cheery little wave and attempted a blithe smile. "Hi," she said lamely.

He cleared his throat, nodded vaguely.

"I—I bet you're surprised to see me," she said, then cringed. *Idiot! Must you remind him of what you walked in on?* She told herself it wasn't her business. She didn't own him. What did she expect, that he would wall himself up in some dungeon with nothing but his personal shrine to Kimberly Norman, counting the days until she called for her next Jax Fix?

He nodded again. "A little bit, yes," he said.

"Well..." With an apologetic smile, she held out her arms in a halfhearted *"ta-da"* pose. "Surprise!"

His brow knit. He didn't speak.

It was odd, but she suddenly realized she'd never really thought about Jax and other women. For as long as she could remember, he hadn't had any one particular girlfriend. He dated, sure, but nobody special. He did mention his partner was a woman, but he neglected to mention she was gorgeous. Bitter resentment washed over her. Did "partner" mean more than mere business between Jax and Tracy? True, the beauty didn't live with Jax, but...she had been *almost* kissing him. *So what?* she admonished inwardly. *Who Jax does and does not kiss is Jax's business, not yours. You must quit obsessing!*

"Actually your secretary said it would be okay if I…" She let the sentence die and shrugged apologetically. "I'm so sorry for bursting in…" She couldn't say it, could hardly bear to think it. Even so, the reality was burned into her brain for all time. "She's quite lovely."

He watched her gravely. "Yes, she is."

Is that all he was going to say? She wanted to know much, much more. Was it serious? Did he love her? Were they planning to get married? Were they casual sex buddies? What exactly was this woman to Jax?

When it was clear he had no plans to say anything more, she couldn't stand it and threw out as nonchalantly as she could manage, "Do I hear wedding bells for you two?"

He folded his arms before him, his gaze so intense she felt its heat. "I'd like to get married—one day," he said. "Tracy isn't keen on the institution, though."

Heavens! She felt diminished, absurdly vulnerable, considering the circumstances. How shallow and silly to be hurt because Jax wanted to marry somebody. Shallow, silly and nuts. So why would she give her eyes if only it had been the other way around—if Tracy craved marriage, but Jax was indifferent about the idea? "Oh?" She struggled to remain nonchalant. "Well, you're a man who gets what he wants," she said. "I have complete faith in you." *To come to your senses!* she shouted inwardly. *I can tell by looking at Tracy, she's not right for you!* She picked an invisible piece of lint off her jacket sleeve, trying to decipher why she'd taken such an instant dislike to Tracy. What had the woman done besides become the object of Jax's desire?

"Actually, I should explain—"

"Nonsense!" Kim cut in. She certainly didn't lust for details. "Your personal life is your business. You're a man. She's a woman. You're partners. It's—it's perfectly—" *Horrible. I hate it!* "—perfect!" she finished clumsily. She had trouble looking at him, so handsome, yet so serious. Finally, in a desperate bid for self-preservation, she dropped her gaze and turned to scan a bookcase filled with hardbacks.

Needing to move, she strolled toward it, pretending to examine the books. "Actually I was working on the entertainment for the spouses when I thought I'd drop by for a tour of your offices." She ran a finger along the volumes, not actually seeing them. Her mind's eye refused to relinquish the sight of Jax and Tracy practically in flagrante.

What if she had burst in a minute later? Would they have been sprawled on his desk going at it like rabbits? Her stomach turned over and she started hyperventilating again. She sucked in a big breath then let it out. *Breathe slowly! Breathe slowly!* "But, now…" She made an extravagant show of checking her watch. "I see it's later than I'd realized. I need to get going. Things to do, you know." She managed to face him, smiling desperately hard. She held out her hands to indicate his office, plush, golden carpeting, high-end, contemporary oak furnishings, magnificent view. "It's beautiful. Really beautiful."

"Thanks." His expression showed precious little enthusiasm. Sadly for Kim, he looked urbane and sexy standing there, even though his arms were folded in a classic pose of rejection. His white dress shirt and dark woolen trousers fit him flawlessly. That bad boy curl mocked from its chosen berth just above finely arched eyebrows.

"You're welcome," she said. "It was nothing. Nothing at all." She displayed an indifference she was far from feeling. His brusque manner unsettled her, and the lingering lulls in conversation became oppressive. She usually felt at ease with Jax, but not today. Plainly her interruption aggravated him, having been denied his carnal gratification.

Maybe last night he hadn't had a toothache, after all. Maybe he had only been hot for Tracy. *Clearly my impromptu visit cut deeply into his sex life, whether he willingly admits it or not.* Her face felt fiery and she prayed she wasn't blushing. "Well…I'll be going." She spun away, then recalled one of the reasons she came by and looked back. "I'm going to run by the supermarket. Any requests for supper?"

"I'm not sure what time I'll be home. Don't go to any trouble."

She wanted to shout, *You're no trouble, Jax. If you want truffles and baklava, I'll fix them for you. You're my best friend. I'd do anything for you. Don't you understand? I love you!* but she only nodded. "Whatever you say." Self-conscious and unsettled, she gave one last, huge effort to appear cheery. "I'll see you—when I see you?"

"Right."

She fumbled with the strap of her shoulder bag, hoping he would say something, but unsure what she wanted to hear. When he remained silent, she knew she had to move or chance having him see through her facade, which she dared not allow. She couldn't even explain her feelings to herself. She nodded. "Okay, then…" She swallowed, turned away, abandoning her smile. "Bye," she called, heading out his office door.

He never said goodbye.

Jax watched Kim leave well aware of what she thought had been going on between him and Tracy. And his oh-so-hilarious partner hadn't made things any better with her flippant innuendos. *All play and no work!* When she said that he almost vaulted over his desk to strangle her. Somehow he managed to keep his cool. Barely.

He almost told Kim the truth—that Tracy had been reaching past him for a stack of files when a loop of yarn on her shaggy, designer jacket caught on his shirt button. When Kim walked in he'd been trying to get them untangled. And Tracy, as usual, had been her mischievous self, making things difficult simply to harass him. Trace was a fine business partner, but as a jester she sucked.

He opened his fist to let a small, white shirt button drop to his desktop. The tiny sound it made seemed like a sonic boom in the stillness. Maybe he should have tried harder to explain. But when Kim interrupted, he'd let it go. If she didn't care, why bother?

He stared at the button, shining white against the dark oak. He felt weary and leaned forward to place his fingertips on the desktop. Closing his eyes, he exhaled heavily.

Every time he saw Kim his emotions were dealt a blow. And today, she suddenly appeared in that slim green, silk suit. Her red hair loose, aflame around her lovely face, and that cruelly intimate dazzle of her smile. The thrill of finding her there affected him so deeply he had trouble forming coherent thoughts. His power of speech withered, leaving him a dumbstruck, mumbling fool.

CHAPTER SIX

KIM felt blackjacked. She had a headache, suffered from dizziness, had difficulty forming thoughts. Since arriving back at Jax's condo, she even had a bout or two of shortness of breath and her heart beat like she just finished a marathon. She dropped to the sofa, wondering what plague she caught in Jax's office. Whatever name it went by, it was totally and instantly debilitating.

She sighed aloud, refolded the cold washcloth covering her eyes and, for the thousandth time, tried to blot out the sight of Jax, smiling—laughing—*touching*—that—that *partner.* She rubbed her temples, wishing she had the power to dig inside her brain, find the bit of gray matter that insisted on reviewing that scene over and over, yank it out, ax it to bits and burn it to ash.

She heard someone crying and recognized the sounds of choking sobs and incoherent mumbling. Jolted, she became aware that the mourning came from her own throat. She bolted upright, an unbearable truth striking her so hard she howled a denial. "No—oh, *please!* No!"

She shook her head, pressed the wet washcloth against her mouth to stifle the sobs and any unwarranted declaration that might escape. She didn't dare put into words the wayward, unwanted insight that exploded inside her brain. She didn't dare allow herself to speak it aloud. In vain, she tried to erase it from her brain, but it reverberated, ricocheted and battered, unrelenting and awesome. "No—*no*…" She dropped the cloth to her lap. "I can't be in love with Jax!"

She gasped and slapped her hands over her offending lips. The worst had happened. She let the scandalous words slip out. Panicking, she looked around, as though the very walls might betray her and echo the confession to their owner.

Jax!

Defeated by the truth, she dropped her hands to her lap, grasped the washcloth and twisted it fretfully. "Jax," she whispered with trembling reverence. "Oh—Jax, I can't be…" No, she would not voice it again. Loving Jax *that way* was too—too—impossible. He was her best friend, her confidant. He could never be her lover.

People lost lovers.

She slumped forward. "I can't lose you, Jax," she cried. "I won't love you that way." She took a deep breath for control, then another. That's right. That's what she had to concentrate on, keeping Jax in the right compartment in her heart. The Best Friend compartment. That way she could keep him forever.

But never, ever could he be her lover, because lovers fought, and lovers parted. The idea of never seeing Jax again made her feel sick. "I can't lose you," she whispered. "Sex changes things. It makes people vulnerable, possessive, mistrustful and bitter. They fight. Love turns to hate." She shuddered at the memory of the knock-down-drag-out-battles she'd witnessed throughout her life. Her mother had been gooey in love one month, then by the next, corrosive hatred spewed from her every pore, and the man was out, never to be seen or heard from again. Her own father left when Kim was barely three. She couldn't remember him at all.

"I can't let that happen between us, Jax," she whispered brokenly. "Without you I'd shrivel up and die."

She experienced a sudden, blinding urgency. "I've got to leave." She jumped up, tossing the washcloth on the coffee table. "I must go home, *now,* before I do anything to betray myself." She ran to the staircase and started up. Halfway to the top, she paused, her promise to Jax nagging. She'd said she would be his hostess. "Oh…dear…" She grabbed the banister, drooped against it. What was she to do? If she left she would be leaving Jax and Tracy in the lurch. Friends didn't do that to friends.

"Of course, they can always hire a hostess," she mumbled. She started up the stairs again, but her steps were plodding and weighed down by guilt. *Kimberly Norman, you told Jax you'd be thrilled to help,* she reminded herself. *Besides, didn't he let you into his home without any notice? Hasn't he always been there for you, whether it was convenient or not?*

Yes, she argued internally, *but he wasn't in love with you. Being around you isn't rocking his emotional boats. It's you who's in danger of drowning.*

She covered her eyes with a shaky hand. "What am I going to do?" *If you leave, Kim,* she warned, *you're a coward. A quitter. A person who goes back on a promise.* She winced. *Don't you have any intestinal fortitude? Just because Jax's "afternoon amour" with Tracy made you face the truth of how you feel, doesn't mean you can't endure another week near him.*

She swiped at a tear. She loved Jax Gideon, not as a friend, but as a fully functioning woman. How many years had she fought that truth? If she were totally honest, she probably knew, deep down, most of her life. Was she so weak she couldn't keep her emotions in check long enough to do him this favor, considering all the favors he'd done for her?

"After next week you can go back to St. Louis and—and

start dealing with your feelings, get them arranged in a manageable form," she lectured under her breath. "Then you'll just have to be more circumspect about your contacts with him. Write him letters, phone him, but stay out of reach."

Something inside her was so sad she had to struggle to keep from doubling over, folding up, right there on the staircase, and crying her heart out. Because the secret, ill-fated woman inside her could no longer hide from the bleak knowledge of her incompleteness, no longer shut out her craving, her desire, her hunger to be held in Jax's arms, like the lover she wanted to be.

But she *couldn't* allow herself to lie down and give in to her emotions. She had to hide her weakness and heartache. She forced herself to straighten to her full height. If she let her sadness have its head, she would have to take to her bed and sob for heaven only knew how long.

"No!" She steeled herself against allowing that buried, wailing woman to take charge. "Weakness would offer me temporary bliss, true. But in the long run, I would lose far more than my heart could bear." Her voice broke, becoming a frayed whisper. "I would lose Jax."

Kim woke with a start and looked at her bedside clock. Two-thirty. She yawned, provoked with herself. She finally fell asleep less than an hour ago, and something had to wake her. She knew it couldn't be Jax getting home because he returned around eleven. She heard the garage door open and close, heard sounds below her bedroom in the kitchen. Heard his footfalls on the stairs some time later as he went to bed. That must have been around midnight. She tossed and turned until after one-thirty when she finally fell into a fitful sleep. "Oh, great," she groused. "Practically a whole hour."

Yawning again, she sat up, realizing she was hungry. She'd

been too upset to eat earlier, and too busy all day getting things set up for Jax's and Tracy's upcoming conclave. If she remembered right, she'd subsisted on one greenish banana and decaf coffee. "It might as well have been full strength," she mumbled, as she slipped on the silky robe matching her beige nightgown. Though silk, the fabric was dense enough for a quick run to the kitchen in the middle of the night. Bright light might show off more than modesty dictated, but shadows and dim lighting would be fine. Especially since she didn't plan on entertaining the troops—or, more to the point, one perilously attractive man occupying the master bedroom across the hall.

Slipping on her scuffs, she quietly exited her room and headed to the stairs. She didn't expect to see illumination in the living room below, but when she reached the staircase, she noticed a fire burned in the hearth. Even more surprising, she could see Jax. He sat on the sofa, hunched forward, forearms resting on his thighs as he stared into the flames. All he had on was a pair of gray sweatpants. Kim stared, unmoving.

The fire did amazing things to the muscle definition in his torso, arms and back. And, as usual, that sexy curl rode his forehead, goading and manipulating her heart.

She couldn't imagine what might be preying so on his mind that would cause him this middle-of-the-night, firelight vigil. Was his meeting with the Japanese businessmen so cataclysmic it could tie a man like Jax into knots, making him lose sleep?

She watched him reverently, every supple curve and plane of his body, fearing herself, afraid for her heart. Yet, her compassion and affection for him would not allow her to turn and run. If she could help, she must. "Jax?"

He blinked, seeming to come back from wherever he'd gone. He turned, following the sound of her voice. Their eyes met when he found her at the head of the staircase. She made herself smile encouragingly. "Is something wrong?"

He'd been frowning and continued to do so. Running a hand through his hair, he stood. "Did I wake you?"

She shook her head. "I don't think so." She grasped the banister to help compensate for the weakening of her knees, and began to descend. "I woke up hungry. Did you get any dinner?"

He shrugged those magnificent shoulders. The fluid beauty stunned the breath out of her. She clutched harder at the banister to remain on her feet, grateful she'd had the presence of mind to grab it.

"I had—something. I think." He shook his head, as though he couldn't remember whether he ate or not.

She reached the carpeting and smiled sympathetically. Leave it to Jax to forget whether he ate or not. His ability to become so absorbed in a project he could forget whether he'd slept or eaten was one of his most endearing traits. Funny, except for his ability to be totally caught up in something, the geeky loner she knew back in school had disappeared. Jaxon Gideon had matured into a breathtaking example of manhood, which wasn't making her effort to do her part as his best friend any easier. She summoned all her strength and walked to him, taking his hand. "Come on. Let's go fix us a couple of roast beef sandwiches. How does that sound?"

He didn't follow her like a lost and hungry mongrel. She turned back, gave him a serious look and tugged harder on his fingers. "Come on. You're a big boy…" Oh, Lord! Did she have to remind herself of how sexy and big and manly he was? She coughed, cleared her throat. "…Er…and you need to keep up your strength." She broke eye contact to preserve her poise. Looking into those brown eyes put a strain on her control, made her weak for him. Bad mistake.

Still clutching his hand, she headed toward the kitchen. This time he followed. She decided to keep up a stream of light chatter. That would help her keep from thinking things she shouldn't think. "My day was certainly eventful. I'm sure you'll be happy about the plans I've made for the Japanese wives. There are a couple of outings I've got on tap for everybody. A little time away from work relieves stress and clears the cobwebs. And with the budget you gave me, well, the sky is practically the limit, I'm happy to say." As she talked she occasionally glanced at him, making sure to look only at his throat. Once, however, she allowed her gaze to slip to his chest. A blunder. She lost her train of thought and stammered to a stop.

"We're going to dinner and to see a chest?" Jax asked, clearly baffled. He flipped on the kitchen lights.

Oh, Heaven! She averted her face to hide her blush, opting to bluff her way through her Freudian slip. "No, a *show,* silly." She released his fingers and scurried to the refrigerator, hoping poking her head inside it would cool her burning cheeks. "You sit down and I'll take care of everything. Do you want something to drink? Tea? Water?"

"I'll get it."

He sounded ominously close—within inches of her backside. She didn't dare check. "No, you won't. You're tired." She waved him toward the table, keeping her head hidden behind the refrigerator door.

"So are you."

She sighed, closed her eyes. This wasn't going well. He could be terribly stubborn. Rather than debate the point, she grabbed the container with the leftover roast and carefully turned around. With the glass dish between them, she felt safer—from herself. At least she couldn't do anything crazy with her hands. "Okay," she said, paying strict attention to his

Adam's apple. "If you insist, you can get the fixings and bread. I'd love a glass of tea."

He said nothing, so she went about slicing thin pieces of beef for the sandwiches. Neither spoke for several minutes. Kim felt uncomfortable in the silence. It allowed her mind to wander far and wide, across topics best ignored. She squeezed her eyes shut, scolding herself silently about such wayward thinking, especially when Jax was inches away. *"Ouch!"* she cried.

"What happened?"

"Stupid! Stupid! *Stupid!*" She stuck a bloody finger in her mouth.

"You cut yourself?"

She nodded, sucking on the wound.

"Well, quit that." Jax took her hand and drew her finger from her mouth. "Let me look at it."

"It's—it's nothing." Blood billowed and ran down her finger to her palm.

"You could use a couple of stitches. I'd better get you to Emergency."

"Don't be silly!" She yanked from his grip and deposited the finger back in her mouth, mumbling around it, "It's fine. I just need a bandage."

"You need stitches." He grabbed a paper towel off a nearby dispenser and wrapped her finger with it. "We're going to the hospital."

She pulled free again. "You can if you want, but I'm not." She had no intention of going anyplace. "I've cut myself worse than this and never had stitches," she said. "Besides, you're a fine one to talk. Mr. 'I-don't-have-a-broken-arm!' Then a week later when you were in so much pain you couldn't put your coat on it was, 'Okay—maybe I do.'" She grabbed another paper towel and wiped up the blood drops that had fallen to the granite counter.

"I was twelve years old and a stubborn blockhead. You're a grown woman who should know better."

"I do know better. I need antiseptic and a bandage."

"Do I have to carry you?"

"When you resort to brute force, you know you're wrong," she scoffed.

"When you faint from blood loss, you'll know who was wrong."

"Okay." She spun toward the kitchen door. "If you won't get me a bandage and antiseptic, I'll do it. Thanks so much."

"Oh, sit down," he said. "I'll get them."

She happened to be next to one of the kitchen chairs, so she sat. "Finally! The quicker you get me those things, the quicker we can go back to making sandwiches."

He glowered at her. "I still say, stitches—"

"*Shut up*, Jax. I mean it." She was so annoyed with herself she wanted to scream. *How dumb can you be, Kim? Using a knife with your eyes closed?* The sooner she could direct his attention elsewhere, the better. "Just get the antiseptic and bandage and *shut up*."

He clamped his jaws. She could see how frustrated he was by the way the muscles bunched in his cheeks. After a minute, he shook his head and snorted his disgust. He moved up beside her, grasped her by the wrist and lifted her injured hand. "At least hold it above your heart until I get back."

She winced. "I will! I will. Just go." She compressed the paper towel wrap tighter over the wound to stop the bleeding. "I'm not your kid, you know!"

"And I'm *not* your damn father," he called back, sounding less cross than—what word was she groping for? Resentful? Weary? Sad? That thought confused her. Sad? Surely not. Maybe she was dizzy. Seeing blood did that to her sometimes, especially her own. She looked under the paper towel. Just a slow ooze now. She replaced it and squeezed, then propped her elbow on the top edge of the chair-back. "It's above my heart," she grumbled to an empty kitchen. "Happy now, Jax?"

No, he wasn't happy. He hadn't been when she first saw him staring into that fire. To top it off, because of her own stupidity and fear of needles, she picked a fight with him when he only had her best interest at heart. Exasperated with her foul, quick temper, she let go of the paper towel and pinched herself hard on the arm. "Take *that* for being such a witch."

Jax was having a dandy day. First, the weirdness with Tracy and Kim in his office, and now, just when he's so hot for Kim he can't sleep and has to stare into the fire like a catatonic mental patient, who shows up, fluttering down the stairs like a sexy angel?

"You are totally screwed, man." He grabbed alcohol, cotton balls and a box of bandages from his medicine cabinet. "Totally screwed." On his way out of his bathroom, he caught the irony of that remark and let go with a caustic laugh. "Poor word choice." He headed down the stairs. "You're not so much screwed as punished—like some sinister, subtle water torture. A constant drip, drip, drip that slowly, steadily drives you insane."

He swung into the kitchen, again hit full force by how lovely Kim was, even with the aggravated frown marring her forehead. All that beautiful red hair, artfully disarrayed from sleep. And that blasted, off-white outfit. He could swear he could see—*things*—or at least shadows of things—womanly swells and hollows. *Drip. Drip. Drip.* The torture dragged on.

"Here." He pulled a chair in front of her. "Give me your hand."

She did as he asked without arguing. He removed the towel and was relieved to see the blood flow had almost stopped.

"See," she said. "I told you."

He gave her a look that he hoped suggested stitches would still have been a good idea, but he didn't say it. The sooner he got her out of sight, the better. "Hold it up." He dabbed antiseptic on a cotton ball.

"That's going to sting," she said.

He raised an eyebrow to suggest she hush if she didn't want to be bodily dragged to the hospital.

"Okay, okay." She squeezed her eyes shut in preparation for the pain.

He swabbed the wound and heard her sharp intake of breath. "Sorry."

She continued to hold her flinching expression until he smoothed the bandage on. "There."

She opened her eyes. "Okay, now we can get back to the sandwiches."

She started to get up but he halted her with a hand on her shoulder. "I'll do it. I don't want blood in mine." Mainly he didn't want her flouncing around in that flimsy thing she had on.

"Jax," she said, sounding a little puny. "On second thought, I'm not hungry anymore."

He peered at her. She looked pale. "Are you going to be sick?" he asked, returning to her side. It took all of his self-discipline not to touch her hair, caress her cheek.

She shook her head. "No, but I—I think I'll go back to bed." She started to get up, swayed and sat down hard. "Oh…" she groaned.

"The sight of your blood made you queasy." It wasn't a question.

She nodded, placing her elbows on the table and her head in her hands.

He should have known. She was never good at dealing with blood. Especially hers.

Somewhere in the ebb and flow of his emotions, anger, frustration, lust, despair and sadness, he experienced the all too familiar one he couldn't, wouldn't resist—his abiding love for her. "Okay, let's go to bed."

She didn't look up when he made that flagrant slip. If she could ignore it, he would. Without another word, he lifted her from her chair. She gave him a wistful smile, encircled his neck with an arm and laid her head against his throat. "I'm such a wimp," she whispered.

He inhaled the scent of her hair; it burned sweet and sexy all the way down. His throat ached. Words were impossible to form, so without speaking he walked out of the kitchen with his soft burden, on through the dining and living rooms, then up the stairs. Kim's body pressed into his. Those shadows beneath her gown became blatantly real. Every nerve his body registered, with cold-blooded precision, the bounty of the woman in his arms.

Drip, drip, drip.

He looked straight ahead, thought of—rather tried to think of—other things, tried not to groan audibly, tried to remain upright, though a crushing need to double over with desire rode him hard.

At long last they reached her door. Though her eyes had been closed, apparently she remained aware of where they were, because she opened them, turned the doorknob and pushed open the door. She turned toward him, smiled, took his face between her hands and pressed her lips to his.

The contact so startled him, he froze as she gifted him with a warm, lingering kiss. When it was done, she lifted her mouth away, whispering, "Good night, Jax," and slid from his arms.

A moment later her door clicked shut.

He didn't know how long he stood there, in the darkness, as still as death. A minute or an eon. When he finally recovered from the shock, he had an urge to kick her door in, stalk to her bed and—and—*"Damn,"* he ground out. "Don't be an ass!" He spun away and lurched down the stairs toward the flickering fire.

It was nothing compared to the inferno raging in his gut, his brain, his heart. When he reached the bottom of the staircase, he cried through a moan, "Why in Hades did you have to do that, Kim?" He fisted his hands, straining for composure. "Why?" Self-discipline exhausted, he sank to his knees.

CHAPTER SEVEN

"WHY in heaven's name did I kiss Jax?"

Kim closed her eyes, berating herself for the millionth time in the past two days—and nights. What possessed her? She remembered feeling queasy and a little dizzy from her cut finger. Jax picked her up and carried her to her room. She opened the door, then—apparently she went insane. Because the next thing she knew, she was kissing Jax *on the lips.*

She'd kissed him before, but not directly on the mouth. She'd pecked his cheeks and his jaw a thousand times. Once, she even kissed him on his nose, when he was sitting down and she could reach it. But never on his lips. She recalled he almost kissed her in high school, after one of their rare dates. Sensing his intention, she had sidestepped his attempt, fearing the repercussions, knowing a romance between them would eventually put an end to a friendship she treasured.

So why the kiss, Kimberly? she silently chided. *Now that you know how dangerous it is! Are you some kind of masochist? You know you're weak for him. What if you let yourself—you know?* In her mind's eye she watched the "you know" play out. The idea of Jax making love to her took her breath away. Her cheeks grew fiery. She touched them. By comparison, her hands felt like blocks of ice.

"Is something wrong?"

Jax's question brought her back to where they were. She sat beside him in his restored '53 Jaguar XK, speeding to his country house. Though the Japanese businessmen and their wives wouldn't arrive until Monday, Jax wanted her to go out early to become familiar with the layout of his home and to let her meet his staff, allowing time for her to tie up loose ends for her hostessing duties.

Tracy would join them on Sunday, which was plenty soon enough for Kim, even though she knew, logically, that with Jax's office romance buddy on the premises, she would be in less danger of pulling another stupid stunt like that kiss.

"Kim?" Jax coaxed, sounding concerned about her mental state.

She turned, trying to appear casually inquisitive. "What?" Maybe she should apologize for kissing him out of the blue like that. *No.* she scolded mentally. *Why bring it up? After all, he didn't kiss you back. Hardly reacted at all.* She imagined he was embarrassed for her, so why embarrass them both by bringing it up?

"Are you okay?" he asked. "Your face is red. Is the car too warm?"

She pretended nonchalance, which wasn't easy while she blushed furiously. "I—it's—probably—yes, it is warm in here." She couldn't come up with another plausible reason for the flush. At least not one she cared to let him in on.

He turned down the heater. "I'm sorry. Why didn't you say something."

She shifted to stare out of the window at rolling hills of wooded land, bedecked in a crazy-quilt of autumn colors. Here and there fields of soybeans or corn took center stage, ripe and ready for the harvest. Cattle and horses grazed in tranquil pastures. Farm houses and big, old weathered barns dotted the landscape, quaintly bucolic. The provincial panorama helped calm her. After several minutes, she felt her pulse beat slow to an almost normal rhythm. "How much further, Jax?" she asked.

"Not much."

She started to face him, then thought better of it, and continued to stare out of the window. "The trees are so much more colorful here than in Chicago."

"Sunlight's intensity is reduced by smoke and dust particles in the city."

"Oh?" Jax was so smart about everything. His ability to draw facts seemingly from thin air always amazed her. "Whatever the reason, it's beautiful."

"I liked it when I saw it."

He drew her attention against her will and better judgment. She turned toward him. "Your country home must be huge, since you can handle so many guests," she said. "Why did you buy such a big place you hardly ever use?"

He peered at her for a split second, too short to make out the look in his eyes. But she had a sensation of sadness before he returned his gaze to the road. "Five years ago I almost got married."

That news struck Kim like a baseball bat to the back of her head. A full minute passed before she could speak. "You? Married?"

He kept his eyes on the road, nodded. "Almost."

"Really?" Kim found this news hard to take. "So—so why didn't you?"

He flinched, pursed his lips. Clearly this "almost marriage" wasn't a subject he relished discussing. Still, she couldn't bring herself to say, "Never mind, it's none of my business." She knew she *should* say it, and sensed Jax *wanted* her to say it. But she clamped her jaws shut, needing to know about this "almost marriage," and more importantly his "almost bride."

When her silence made it obvious she had no plans to allow him a gracious out, he cleared his throat. "It didn't work out." He shrugged. "But I kept the place." Glancing her way briefly, he added, "I hope, one day, to raise a family there."

The idea of Jax raising children—some other woman's and his—made her blood run cold. She shivered and hugged herself.

He must have seen her because his frown deepened and he asked, "Are you cold now?"

She felt like an idiot with her body temperature yo-yoing all over the place. First fever, then chills, like a malaria victim. Good Heavens, she had Love Malaria! She shook her head, not merely to answer Jax's question with a mute lie, but to deny even to herself that she had any such ridiculous sickness. She couldn't, *wouldn't* have it. "I'm fine." Uncrossing her arms, she folded her hands in her lap, adopting an image that patently stated, *I am calm, cool and Love Malaria-free.*

"We're here."

Relief swept over her. Sitting so close to Jax for the past hour had taken a nasty emotional toll. "Great." She didn't hide her enthusiasm for reaching the end of their drive. She wanted to put distance between them that the lean, low Jaguar didn't permit.

Jax turned off onto a shady, wooded driveway that wound through a dense stand of white oaks, bathed in dark red foliage, a scattering of saffron sassafras trees and crimson maples. As they rounded a turn, a Mediterranean style mansion appeared atop a knoll. Its stucco exterior gleamed with a buff patina, softened in places by a mantle of manicured vines. Graceful arches abounded and the authentic, red tile roof dazzled in the afternoon sunshine. The home's design and its natural environs blended into a visual feast that was both elegant and comfortable.

The subtlety of the landscaping tricked the eye, making it seem as though the flowers and shrubbery had grown naturally around the home, a work of nature's bounty rather than some high-priced landscaper's design. She smiled in spite of her anxiety. Leave it to Jax to have a perfect mansion. She heard herself giggle, the sound a little on the hysterical side. Quickly she clamped her lips together.

"Why the laugh?" he asked.

She shook her head, working at control. When she felt she had a handle on herself, she said, "It's just so—perfect, it's funny."

He didn't respond as he drove up the knoll and around to the side of the home. A single door of a four car garage rose up and he pulled inside. "Perfection makes you laugh, does it? I don't recall that about you."

She hated herself for allowing the hysterical giggle. She slid out of the car before he had a chance to be a gentleman. Once standing, she made a show of stretching as he unfolded himself from the driver's seat. When he met her gaze over the Jag's teardrop roofline, she continued to stretch, hoping she looked like an indolent cat rather than a nervous wreck. "Sure, perfection makes me laugh."

"Why?" he asked.

Why indeed? She needed a clever, believable lie, and she needed it now. "Well—because perfection—is so—so rare, it makes you smile." Good so far. "And—and smiling is just a sound effect away from laughter."

He seemed to be waiting for her to go on, so she forged blindly ahead. "And—sometimes when a person, place or thing makes me smile, if that person, place or thing is exceptional in some way, it lights my laugh fuse and—bingo—I laugh. Simple enough?" *Laugh fuse? Lights my laugh fuse?* She held eye contact with difficulty. She couldn't believe she'd actually said "laugh fuse," and had to bite her tongue to keep from apologizing for it.

He said nothing, simply stared, so to back up her flaky motivation, she smiled, then laughed. The sound she made wasn't very genuine, but in her defense, being stared down by a gorgeous hunk in a torso-hugging navy sweater—a hunk you were trying desperately not to be in love with—made realistic laughter awkward to pull off. "See? I did it again."

"Why? Is my garage perfect?"

She wanted to say, *No. Your chest is, and that dratted sweater is making it all too plain.* Instead she said, "Yes, your garage is perfection." She was no expert on garages, and she hadn't paid any attention to this one, so she scanned the space. Two other cars, rather a pickup truck and a Jeep, were parked nearby. An empty stall separated the other vehicles and Jax's Jag. Aside from that, the garage consisted of white walls, arched windows and a flagstone floor. She ambled toward the front of Jax's sports car, trailed a finger across a sweeping front fender, pretending to delight in his garage.

"Thank you," he said, impassively. "If you like the garage, I think you'll laugh your head off at the house."

He moved to the trunk and pulled out her suitcase. Since he didn't bring any clothes, Kim assumed he kept some on the premises. After seeing the mansion, she figured there must be precious little this home couldn't deliver—except a wife and kids. On the other hand, how many women who knew Jax at all, and *saw* this home, wouldn't be rabid to accommodate his wife-and-kids project? "You sound pretty confident that I won't loathe the house." She lifted her chin in a teasing gesture. Unless his home was decorated in cow patties and mud, she had no doubts that it would be—well—for lack of a better word—perfection. "Don't count your chickens, buddy-boy. I'm a tough house critic." She struggled to keep the banter lighthearted. "Maybe I'm just hot for huge garages." *Hot? Did I have to say hot?*

"Okay, I won't get my hopes up." He circled around in her direction and took her arm. "Let's go break my spirit."

His light touch at her elbow felt magnified in her mind, as though she were chained to him. She couldn't have disengaged herself even if she had free will. His touch made her a part of him, bodily connected. She didn't even feel she needed to breathe as long as he did. Of course, she did need to breathe, which became clear a minute after he took her arm.

She sucked in a shaky breath, striving to get her mind on the interior of Jax's house. As the hostess, she would need to know the layout intimately.

In a daze she met Jax's housekeeper, Maggie—at least she thought Maggie was the name she heard. Her impression of the middle-aged brunette was mainly ruddy cheeks, a cheerful smile and a salt-and-pepper, braided bun on top of her head. Then there had been the cook, a man, the caretaker, another man and a couple of maids. They blurred in her mind. All she could fully register was Jax's touch, his fingers warm and gentle against her skin.

They passed through a granite bedecked kitchen into the formal entry with a sweeping, curved staircase. Beyond that a great room stretched on forever. Kim recalled smatterings of the tour: a vast dining room, an in-home theater and oak espresso bar, eight—or was it nine?—elegant bedrooms, marble baths with fixtures of gold and antique brass, fireplaces, indoors and out. She vaguely recalled dark ceiling beams, hardwood and Spanish tile floors, and a spectacular view of a private lake across the swimming pool.

There was more. Too much more to take in, let alone remember. All she truly knew was that Jax's home was made
for entertaining on a grand scale. A hostess's heaven. Any
woman's heaven.

"You're not laughing."

His remark pulled her out of her dazed state. Or was it the
fact that he had released her arm and set her mental faculties
free? She blinked, gathered her poise and her wits, then shifted
to look at him. It occurred to her that they were back in the
grand entry hall, having just come down from the bedroom
level. They never went up that staircase, so how…? There
must have been a back staircase somewhere. When Jax wasn't
there she would have to take another trek around to get her
bearings. "I—I—um…" She shrugged, looked around, then
lifted her arms in an all-encompassing manner. "It's beautiful," she said. "No kidding, Jax. Your home is—well, it *is* perfect. That 'almost bride' of yours surely didn't reject you
because the house lacked anything."

She frowned, sorry for that last impetuous remark. Jax's
face had gone uncharacteristically pale. She prayed for the
earth to open up and swallow her. "Oh—I'm so sorry. I
shouldn't have mentioned…" *You're not going to say it again,
are you?* she scolded silently.

"Never mind," he said. "For the record, the house wasn't
the problem."

"Well, of course not. The house is—the house is…"

"Perfect?" he asked, an edge in his tone.

Something in his eyes, something fierce and bitter flum-
moxed her. She couldn't think, couldn't speak. She stared off,
almost sick for being so insensitive. To get the look in his eyes
out of her head she concentrated on the great room. For the
first time she noticed that washed river rock had been incor-
porated into walls, columns and the fireplace. Not that she

gave a flying flip about washed river rock, but it was something to center on while she tried to regain her composure, find the right words. Her mind turned back to his odd, unsettling stare, and tears welled up. She blinked them back.

"Would you like to freshen up?" he asked.

"Oh, yes." She blinked furiously. "I think—thank you." He was sweet to forgive her for her faux pas. Jax was like that. He could disregard thoughtless blunders and move on. When she regained control, she managed a grateful smile. "I'm afraid I forgot which room was mine."

"I'll have Maggie show you."

A moment later he was gone. Could she blame him when she'd all but suggested he was such a loser that even with this beautiful home he couldn't get a woman to marry him. Which hadn't been her intent at all. It had to have been Jax who decided against the marriage. He must have come to understand that his "almost bride" wasn't good enough for him. "And I'm sure she *wasn't*," she mumbled.

"Ma'am?"

Kim whirled to see a middle-aged woman with a braided bun and ruddy cheeks. "Oh—Maggie, is it?"

"Yes." She smiled. Maggie was an attractive woman, even without a drop of makeup. She wore a black dress with a white lace collar that suited her demure style. Or was it a uniform? Whatever, she wore black well. Her shoes were sensible, stylish pumps. "Jax said you wanted to freshen up." Maggie indicated the staircase with a sweep of her arm. "Right this way."

Kim fell into step behind the woman, wondering what it must be like to be in charge of a house that had to be fifteen-thousand square feet of cutting-edge luxury and Old World charm, especially considering its owner was hardly ever there. But, she wasn't here to let her mind drift and wander to irrelevant topics. "Maggie," she said, "we need to get together soon so you can fill me in on meals, schedules, things like that. We need to coordinate. I'm sure Jax told you I'm to be his official hostess to keep the wives occupied."

"Yes, ma'am."

"Please, call me Kim."

"Thank you." At the top of the stairs Maggie paused and faced Kim. "Dinner will be served at seven. Perhaps sometime this evening, at your convenience?"

"I imagine that will be fine, if it doesn't interfere with Jax's plans. I'm not sure what we might—"

"Oh, he left."

Maggie's statement didn't register at first. When it sank in, Kim felt like she'd been slapped. She closed her eyes and took a breath before asking, "Left?"

"Yes. I believe he went back to the city. He said something urgent came up."

Urgent in the last three minutes? Kim knew what came up that was so urgent. Her tactless mouth, that's what. She had opened up a wound. Oh, how she loathed herself. Nodding, she said, "I see. So—it's just me for dinner?"

"Yes."

Depressed, she blew out a breath, continuing to nod on the outside but kicking herself black and blue on the inside. "Well—fine. Then we can talk any time, it seems."

She had a sudden, awful thought. Could it be that Jax's rushed return to Chicago was less "urgent" than "urge?"

As Maggie showed Kim to her room, lurid visions of Tracy and Jax—their arms and legs entwined in silken sheets, feverish and flushed—blinded her with jealousy. When Maggie turned to go, Kim shut herself inside her room and sagged against the door, sucking air into oxygen-starved lungs. It hurt to breathe almost as much as it hurt to think of Jax and...well, it hurt.

* * *

Jax woke with a start, shivered and realized it had grown dark. Apparently his exhausting swim in the hidden cove had done what no amount of tossing and turning could do. He'd pulled himself out of the water and fallen on soft grass in the sunlit bower, and finally fallen into a deep sleep.

But now it was dark, and the air had turned chilly. He was accustomed to nude, cold swims out here, in the peace and quiet of his private lake. This inlet lay concealed from the house by dense woodland. He'd discovered it once when entering his property from a back road, then driving his Jeep overland. No one else knew about this spot or that he came here. It had become his place of solace, his place to go and think, to swim and relax away the strains of business. Or like today, he could exhaust himself swimming, climb ashore and fall into a deep enough sleep where even dreams could not go.

Kim's questions about his "almost bride" rattled him, reminded him of that difficult chapter in his life. He sat up, bent his knees in order to rest his forearms across them and clasped his wrists. He hadn't thought about Marilyn in a long time. He hated what he'd done to her by lying to himself. Telling himself that her resemblance to Kimberly was mere coincidence. That he was not trying to find a substitute for Kim in Marilyn. But the eve before their wedding invitations were to be mailed, he knew the attempt would fail, and to go through with a marriage based on a lie was doomed.

He told Marilyn the truth, but he also told her that since he asked her to marry him, and she answered yes, in good faith, the choice was hers. He would honor his commitment if that was what she wanted—knowing the truth.

He lowered his head to rest on his forearms. Of course she broke it off. Marilyn was a kind, bright woman, who didn't hold herself so cheap that she would cling to a man who didn't love her in the deep, forever way she deserved. He hurt her badly, and he still suffered for that. But last year, she called, told him she forgave him and that she was getting married, was blissfully happy, and she wished him happiness, too.

But his "almost bride" had taught him a hard lesson. Finding a substitute for Kim was wrong. Getting Kim out of his heart was the answer. And that was his goal. "One more week," he murmured, aching with the despair of inevitability. "I will rid myself of you in one more week. I must." He knew getting her out of his heart wouldn't be easy, but once he told her he wanted her out of his life, then there was a chance he could begin to heal.

He shivered, but only partly from the cold. Feeling like a fool, hunched naked in the dark woods, he stood, started toward his Jeep, then paused and turned. Unsure why, he walked through the trees until he could see his house, high on the knoll. He checked his watch, its luminous face clear in the darkness. After ten. Good Lord, how long had he slept? He was lucky the weather was unseasonably warm for the first of October, or he would have pneumonia by now.

He stared up at his house for a long time, the quiet broken only by the funereal *hooo-hooo* of a distant owl, sounding as lonely and melancholy as Jax felt. Golden light poured from arched windows on the main floor in the kitchen and staff's wing. Maggie was reading, as was her habit, and the cook and caretaker were embroiled in their usual game of checkers.

His gaze drifted upward to Kimberly's room, next to his own. All was dark. He had a desperate urge to break into a run across the meadow, up the hill, to climb the wisteria, slip in her window and crawl naked into her bed.

"Just once," he whispered to the night wind. "I would give anything, Kimberly, *anything*—to make love to you. Just once."

CHAPTER EIGHT

OH, GOODY, Tracy's here, Kim thought, standing back as Jax met his partner at the grand double-doored entry. She came in with a flourish and a carefree wave at Kim. Kim waved back halfheartedly while Jax's partner gave him an affectionate hug. "Hi!" she said with a big smile. "Have a nice weekend, you two?"

"It was busy," Jax said. "But I think we have everything worked out."

Kim smiled, nodded. As far as she, Jax and the housekeeper were concerned, all would run smoothly. They'd rearranged a few meals to adjust to Kim's plans for the spouses and the night out to dinner in Chicago and the theater production. Kim had been happy to discover that Maggie was very accommodating and a joy to work with. Which was more than she could say at the moment about Jax.

He'd been there, answered questions, listened to her suggestions, made adjustments in the meeting schedule to coordinate with her plans. But he hadn't been there for her *emotionally*. Every time she'd wanted to be near him, to sit and enjoy his company, he seemed to always find something he had to do right that second. It had been like trying to catch a wild rabbit. One second you saw him, then *poof*, he was gone.

"Say, Jax Man," Tracy said, taking his hand. "I need a chat." She gave Kim a smarmy smirk. "Private. You understand."

Kim was afraid she did. Speaking of rabbits, did those two ever take a break?

"Purely business," Tracy added with a clandestine wink.

"No problem." Kim indicated her clipboard. "I have to—" she blanked out "—work," she finally finished lamely.

"Don't we all." Tracy tugged Jax in her wake. "Oh, Kim, honey, tell Maggie to feed the chauffeur. I'm afraid I kept him running all day."

"Sure," she said to their backs as they disappeared up the staircase to the bedroom floor. Kim wanted to shout, "Exactly why do you have to talk business with Jax in a bedroom when there's a perfectly good office down here?" But she wasn't so naïve she needed to ask such a silly question. "Business-schmisness," she muttered as a husky chauffeur carted in two suitcases. He sat them on the tile floor and gave her a look that suggested he needed directions. "Um—I don't know where they go."

"I'll handle it." Maggie appeared from the direction of the kitchen.

"Oh, and Tracy asked that you feed…" She indicated the chauffeur. "What's your name?"

"Mossy."

"Feed Mossy." She returned her gaze to Maggie. "You probably knew that."

Maggie smiled. "Yes, Mossy and I are old friends." She went to the staircase. "Follow me with those, and then I'll have Cook make you a snack."

The chauffeur, a man in his mid-thirties, a burley, ex-football type, gave Kim a rather impure grin. "Thanks," he said. "And who are you, sweetie?"

"Careful," Maggie said. "She's a close, personal friend of Jax's."

Mossy's grin faded and he made an apologetic face. "Oops. Sorry. I thought you were one of us hirelings." He touched the brim of his uniform cap in a salute of sorts. "Pleasure to meet you."

Kim smiled with effort. In reality, she was a hireling, too, but decided not to go into that, since Mossy seemed willing to become a problem if she gave him half a chance. That's all she needed, an amorous chauffeur on her scent while she pined for a man who was probably flinging off his clothes at this very moment in anticipation of…she squelched the vision. "It's nice to meet you."

"Thank you, ma'am. The name's Mossberg. Andrew Mossberg, but everybody calls me Mossy." He lowered his gaze, now all professional and respectful. Hefting the bags he followed Maggie upstairs. Kim presumed they knew better than to burst in on Jax and Tracy midromp. Maybe for propriety's sake, Tracy had her own room. That was very likely, considering the conservative culture of their guests, who would be arriving within twenty-four hours.

Speaking of that, Kim made herself concentrate on her clipboard. She had last-minute details to deal with, no matter what wild debauchery went on upstairs.

Jax allowed Tracy to pull him into his bedroom. Once the door closed he disengaged her hold on his hand. "Okay, Tracy, what's going on?" He was losing patience. He'd held himself in check all weekend, straining to keep his hands off Kim. He had precious little patience left. "Why are we in my bedroom?"

She plopped down on his king-size bed and lay back, stretching like a spoiled feline. She grinned at him, then scanned the large master suite, with its earth tones and clean, modern lines. "Nice digs," she said. "A little big for one man, don't you think?"

He eyed her with deepening suspicion. "On the other hand, it's way too small for more than one man."

She laughed, pushed up to sit. "You're so hetero it's positively indecent."

"I'm in no mood for your ribbing."

She crossed her arms, her expression scheming.

He aimed a damning finger at her. "I don't like that look."

Her grin broadened. "I've been thinking, Jax." She pushed off the bed and walked to him.

"Damn it, Tracy, I've warned you about that," he said. "I don't trust you when you think."

She clapped him on the upper arms, her grip firm. "This is genius, Jax. Hear me out."

He stared her down. "If this is about Kim, forget it."

"Hey," she said like a stern mother hen. "Just listen. Don't be so pigheaded for once."

"I'm not pigheaded," he said. "If anybody's pigheaded in this twosome, it's you."

"Oh?" she asked with exaggerated drama, her eyes extra wide, her brows hiked to the extreme. "*That,* Jax Man, remains to be seen." She grinned impishly.

Her smirking manner troubled him. What was going on in her crafty head? "Whatever you're thinking, stop it."

"Oh, shut up." She squeezed his arms. "With all your futile protesting, you've churned yourself up for no reason. If you'd just listened to my idea we could be all done now, and you could be hugging me for my magnificent brainwork."

He gave up. "Okay. Get it out of your system," he said. "I have things to do."

She shook her head. "You can be so negative. Anyway, this

is my idea. First of all, you're tired of Kim using you as her rebound man, right?"

He ground his teeth, stared at her hard, then finally admitted it with a reluctant nod.

"Right. So my thought is this. We tell the Japanese folks she's your fiancée. Spring it on her in front of them so she can't object for fear of ruining—"

"Are you out of your *freaking* mind?" He brushed her hands from his arms. "I'm not springing any such thing on Kim." He strode away, stared out of the window-wall with glass doors opening onto the balcony above his pool. "What would be the point?"

"The point would be that if she is to play hostess, it would make more sense if you're an actual couple. I'm afraid our Japanese guests will be insulted if they think we hired somebody to 'babysit' their wives."

He frowned. "That's ridiculous."

"But more important," Tracy went on as though he hadn't spoken, "...as your fiancée, you and she could—well, share this nice big room."

For a second the significance of her suggestion didn't register. When it did, his frown became a glare. "What?"

She wagged her eyebrows, the personification of a wicked imp. "Think of the perks. You could have sweaty sex with her, like you've wanted to for—well, *forever.* Use *her* for a change. Think of it as long overdue payback."

He couldn't believe what he was hearing and ran a hand through his hair, frustrated and growing angry. "Take her against her will? You are certifiable, Trace. You've gone way over the edge this time. They have a name for that, and just in case you haven't heard, it's a major crime."

"No, no!" She hurried toward him, taking his hand in both of hers. "I can read women, Jax, and I swear I'm getting jealousy vibes from her. I believe she has a thing for you, but she's afraid to show it. So I'm thinking, getting you two alone in bed—well—all you'd have to do is your manly, sexy thing." She winked. "Which, I've heard through the grapevine, is quite—er—how shall I put it?"

"Don't!"

"Quite—*satisfying,*" she went on, apparently lost in her own bizarre vision. "Yes, that's the word. Satisfying." She made an extravagant point of shrugging. "If you're into that sort of thing. Anyway, you do your zowie-wowie sex magic. She'll purr like a kitten full of cream all week, and you'll get her out of your system." Tracy nodded curtly, as though confident. "Yes. Most times that, alone, will get somebody out of my system. It's a lust thing, Jax Man. You've been lusting after her so long you can't tell it from love."

Jax listened with a heavy heart, his anger rising.

"Get her into bed and get over her," Tracy insisted, plainly on fire about the grotesque idea. "When the week's up, kick her to the curb. *Finis.* The End. Over and out." She still clutched his hand, her expression full of expectation, as though she believed he would suddenly grasp the brilliance of her plan and shout, *"Eureka! I'll do it!"*

He pulled from her grip and turned away, his long, low exhale muffling a blasphemy. "Tracy, go to—*unpack.*"

"What are you saying, Jax?"

He peered at her over his shoulder. "I'm suggesting you go unpack your suitcases before I lose what little control I have left and toss you through this window so hard you end up orbiting earth as a second moon." He turned his back on her to indicate the discussion was over.

After a moment, she patted his shoulder. "Okay," she said softly. "I'm sensing you want to think it over, so why don't I go unpack?"

"Get the hell *out!*" he growled.

"Sure, sure," she said. "Don't blow a gasket."

He listened to her tread softly across the carpeting. Heard the door open, then close. After a moment, he turned to make sure she was gone, then scanned his bedroom restlessly. Of all the stupid ideas. It wasn't only stupid, it was cruel. Using Kim as a meeting planner was one thing, but using her sexually, then dumping her like yesterday's garbage? That was too cold-blooded even to consider.

But making love to her? He opened the glass doors to the balcony, walked outside and grasped the cold metal railing. A breeze rushed in from the woods, across the lake, fragrant, nutty and cool. He peered down at the pool below, then across the landscaped yard, finally focusing on the lake's glassy surface, fiery in the setting sun. "Kimberly, don't even give me hope of making love to you," he whispered beneath his breath, "or I will."

Kimberly knew the company limousine had returned from the airport and entered the property. She could hear the excited murmurs of the added staff, hired for the week, as the word spread upstairs. She wet her lips, fluffed her hair and straightened the collar of her green silk suit.

She was as ready as she would ever be to meet the Ishikawas, Inoues, Yoshidas, Otakas and Nakamuras. Now if she could only remember to correctly pronounce their names. She'd practiced for the past hour as she went over the social rules, how deep to bow, to remain reserved, polite and not gush or be aggressive, to dress impeccably. There would be no Casual Days this week.

"Whew, now please let me not flub my speech," she said to herself, gathering up the wrapped gifts—golden writing pens for the men and engraved compacts for the wives. "Remember," she murmured. "Gifts are to be presented with both hands and a slight bowing of the head." She picked up one of the packages, held it out with both hands. With a slight bow she said, "Please accept this, er, insignificant remembrance to welcome you on behalf of Gideon and Ross." She straightened, shook her head. "Not perfect." She held out the gift, cleared her throat, and began again. "Please accept—"

A knock on her bedroom door drew her out of her rehearsal. "Yes?"

"The limo's pulling up out front," Maggie called. "You said you want to greet them at the door."

"Oh—absolutely. Thanks." She scooped the gifts into a decorated basket. Hurrying out of her room, she smiled at Maggie as she caught up. "How's the new staff working out so far?"

"They're pros," Maggie said. "We've used them before."

"Ah, right." She hurried on. *Sure! Of course!* What a naïve question. Jax said that they did a lot of company entertaining here. Where was her mind? At the top of the staircase she reminded herself to be calm, dignified. No more sprinting down hallways. She took a breath and began to descend the sweeping staircase, thinking, *Be a queen! Descend like a queen.*

Halfway down, the entry doors swung wide. Mossy, the chauffeur, did the honors on one side while the newly acquired butler, Otto, held the other door. Both men looked classy in their uniforms: Mossy, in gray, and Otto, in black. Both men bowed slightly, and in unison. She felt a real sense of accomplishment at the sight since she'd taken great pains briefing the staff on etiquette for their Asian visitors. Now, she just needed to worry about herself.

As she reached the bottom of the staircase, she could see Jax and Tracy climbing the entry steps with their guests. A quick inspection of the couples revealed that all the men wore dark suits; the women dark, tailored dresses. All looked to be in their late forties to early sixties. Conservatism shimmered off them like heat off the desert.

Silently she repeated their names and her welcoming speech, her smile self-conscious. *And don't stare. They don't like a lot of direct eye contact,* she reminded herself, shifting to focus on power ties and pearl necklaces. Remembering that would be the hardest change for her, since she was a very direct-eye-contact kind of person.

Once the business couples were inside, Tracy ushered them into the great room. The plan was that after being introduced, Kim would give each one a welcoming gift. She noticed Jax excusing himself, then caught sight of Maggie beckoning for his attention. She hoped it was nothing serious, and kept her smile pasted on, holding herself in her most dignified manner. Tracy's hand on her arm startled her. She shifted her attention, curious.

"Is something wrong?" Kim asked.

"What?" Tracy frowned, then seemed to get it. "Oh, you mean Jax? No, it's just a nuisance call from a nervous client he's been babying along. Listen, Kim," she went on in a conspiratorial whisper, "this is a *huge* sacrifice on my part, but considering the conventional nature of our guests—" She broke off, shook her head. "No time to explain, just go along with what I say. It's *vital* to our success." She gave Kim's arm an authoritative squeeze then strode toward the front of the group. Kim stared after her, baffled. What was the huge sacrifice Tracy spoke of making? And what was she to "go along" with that was so "vital" to their success?

"We are delighted to have you all here," Tracy said over the general murmuring. The group quieted, grew attentive. Kim prepared herself for her speech, deciding whatever Tracy had been talking about would become clear. Right now, she had names to remember and gifts to present. She went over

The Harlequin Reader Service® — Here's how it works:

Accepting your 2 free books and gift places you under no obligation to buy anything. You may keep the books and gift and return the shipping statement marked "cancel." If you do not cancel, about a month later we'll send you 6 additional books and bill you just $3.57 each in the U.S., or $4.05 each in Canada, plus 25¢ shipping & handling per book and applicable taxes if any.* That's the complete price and — compared to cover prices of $4.25 each in the U.S. and $4.99 each in Canada — it's quite a bargain! You may cancel at any time, but if you choose to continue, every month we'll send you 6 more books, which you may either purchase at the discount price or return to us and cancel your subscription.

*Terms and prices subject to change without notice. Sales tax applicable in N.Y. Canadian residents will be charged applicable provincial taxes and GST.

If offer card is missing write to: The Harlequin Reader Service, 3010 Walden Ave., P.O. Box 1867, Buffalo, NY 14240-1867

NO POSTAGE
NECESSARY
IF MAILED
IN THE
UNITED STATES

BUSINESS REPLY MAIL

FIRST-CLASS MAIL   PERMIT NO. 717-003   BUFFALO, NY

POSTAGE WILL BE PAID BY ADDRESSEE

HARLEQUIN READER SERVICE
3010 WALDEN AVE
PO BOX 1867
BUFFALO NY 14240-9952

Do You Have the LUCKY KEY?

PLAY THE Lucky Key Game

and you can get

FREE BOOKS
and a FREE GIFT!

Scratch the gold areas with a coin. Then check below to see the books and gift you can get!

YES! I have scratched off the gold areas. Please send me the 2 FREE BOOKS and GIFT for which I qualify. I understand I am under no obligation to purchase any books, as explained on the back of this card.

386 HDL D7Y2   186 HDL D7Z3

FIRST NAME   LAST NAME

ADDRESS

APT.#   CITY

STATE/PROV.   ZIP/POSTAL CODE

2 free books plus a free gift   1 free book

2 free books   Try Again!

Offer limited to one per household and not valid to current Harlequin Romance® subscribers. All orders subject to approval. Credit or Debit balances in a customer's account(s) may be offset by any other outstanding balance owed by or to the customer.

www.eHarlequin.com

DETACH AND MAIL CARD TODAY!

(H-R-10/05)

© 2002 HARLEQUIN ENTERPRISES LTD. ® and ™ are trademarks owned and used by the trademark owner and/or its licens everything in her head while Tracy continued. "Jax and I are pleased for you to meet our charming hostess." Tracy lifted an arm in Kim's direction. "Kimberly *Gideon*, Jax's bride." She moved to Kim's side and took her hand, squeezing hard as she led her to the front. "Jax and Kimberly are delighted to have you as guests in their lovely home."

Tracy smiled at Kim, in a daze, unsure of what she was hearing. It sounded something like Tracy announced that she was *married* to Jax. But that couldn't be. Why would she say such a crazy thing, especially since Tracy and Jax were lovers—or…was this the sacrifice Tracy mentioned? Was this what she was supposed to "go along" with, the thing so "vital" to their success? Why? What could possibly be so important that they would decide to concoct this insane ruse—especially without letting her in on the plan?

She searched for Jax but he hadn't returned. Behind her polite smile Kim gritted her teeth. *Jax, when I get my hands on you!*

"Well, Kimberly, don't you have something for our visitors?" Tracy's question yanked Kim out of her churning emotions. *Oh! My speech! Their names!* Her mind had gone blank. All she could think of was that she had just become Jax's bride in front of ten Japanese citizens. Ten citizens, whom she now noticed wore smiles of congratulations on their faces. Apparently the institution of marriage was as highly esteemed in Japan as it was here. Possibly more so, unless there were many women in Japan, like her mother, the serial bride, who thought so "highly" of marriage, she chalked up as many as she possibly could.

She tried valiantly to smile as she scoured her brain for something to say that vaguely resembled her speech. "Um—" *Think, darn you, Kimberly! Think.* Stepping forward, she decided she had no choice but to trust herself. She'd practiced and practiced. It was time to get the thing said. She knew it by memory, fake marriage or no fake marriage. She put her brain on autopilot giving her speech, bowing, presenting the gifts and pronouncing names. When she concluded, she felt like she'd been on stage for an eternity. But even with her mental turmoil over her abrupt "marriage" to Jax, she somehow got through it.

Out of the corner of her eye, she saw Maggie lurking at the entry, sparking her memory of what came next. She introduced Maggie, and announced that the housekeeper would show the couples to their rooms so they could have time to themselves to freshen up before tea and hors d' oeuvres at four o'clock.

Maggie ushered them toward the staircase. Kim looked around to discover Tracy making a hasty exit out of a door leading to the kitchen. Kim hightailed it after her, wanting answers. She had managed to hide her anxiety over her surprise marriage until now, but only barely. Once in the kitchen, she found Tracy and Jax alone. Jax was hanging up his cell phone. Angry and ready to blow, Kim barreled toward them like a military tank on the attack. "Just what was the idea?" she demanded.

Tracy held up a halting hand. "Wait a second." She turned to Jax. "Remember our discussion yesterday?"

He looked puzzled. "Which one?"

"The one where we discussed how our business guests would be insulted if they thought we'd hired somebody to babysit their wives, and we discussed that it would be better if they thought Kimberly was a real hostess, like—say—your fiancée—or something?"

"I remember." His frown deepened. "Why?"

Kimberly shoved past Tracy and got in Jax's face. "Because, apparently we're *married,* that's why! And *we're* delighted to have them visit *our* home!" She flung a hand toward Tracy. "As if you didn't know, she announced it in front of everybody just now." She shoved hard against Jax's solar plexus. He grunted and staggered a step backward. "How *could* you, Jax?"

His gaze narrowed, shifting from Kimberly to Tracy. "What did you do?" he demanded, his tone low and threatening.

She grinned sheepishly. "I guess I am the pigheaded one, after all. You were right about that."

"I may have to strangle you for this."

Kim's anger mutated to edgy confusion. "Are you saying you didn't agree to this?" she asked him.

"Of course not." The pain in his voice tugged at her heart.

"Well, it's done now," Tracy said, sounding way too cheerful, considering she was in a room full of sharp knives with two people clearly in the mood for murder. "You can't tell them I lied, or they'll think one of us is insane, and out the window will go any chance of getting their business."

"One of us *is* insane," Jax growled.

"Or to put it another way," Tracy quipped, "I made your bed, now you two have to lie in it." She laughed and smacked Jax on the arm in a buddy-buddy gesture. "Personally I think it was a stroke of genius. Our Japanese friends will feel more comfortable believing this is a nice family home inhabited by a happy, married couple. I mean, did you see that group? They remind me of my Kansas roots—conservative heartland and all that. I toyed with the notion of going the fiancé route we discussed, but I decided marrying you two off would be more palatable to their sensibilities."

"It's not palatable to mine," Jax said, nostrils flaring.

"Mine, either!" Kim's emotions were in chaos. She loved Jax, yes, but she didn't like the institution of marriage as she knew it. Love turned to hate. Battles broke hearts, vows and contracts. People split. Of course, this was a farce for a group of business owners and their wives who would be half a world away in a week, but still, even the marriage lie troubled her.

She grabbed Jax's arm. "You can't really think they would be insulted to know I was a hired hostess?"

"Not for a minute," he said, obviously disgusted by his partner's chicanery. "But, Tracy is right about one thing." He glared at the blonde. "They wouldn't touch our service with a ten-foot pole if we tell them she lied now." He turned his back and placed the flats of his hands on the countertop. "You've put us in a fine fix, Trace," he muttered.

"Not at all," she said brightly. "Your room is large. You two can share it perfectly platonically." She paused, cleared her throat then patted Jax's shoulder. "I mean, since you're just *friends*." She faced Kimberly, her expression oddly amused. "Isn't that true? You're just good friends. Right?"

Kim dropped her gaze to her hands, tying themselves into knots. "Yes—right," she said. *We have to be just friends. We have to be!*

"Well, what's the prob, then?" Tracy lifted her eyebrows as though baffled at their angst. "I'm not going to lie to you," she said, now contriving to look more serious. "This is harder on me than you can imagine."

"I can imagine," Jax muttered. He peered over his shoulder to glare at her. "I'm not going to lie to you, Trace. When this thing is over, I plan to—"

"Whoa, Jax, I never noticed that big, throbbing vein in your neck before." She began to back away. "I'll go tell Maggie to move Kim's things."

"Don't, Tracy, please," Kim said, appalled.

"Silly girl, you're married." Tracy swung her arms out in an expansive gesture. "Married people don't have separate bedrooms. Think, girl. Think." She poked a finger at her head, then grinned and pointed at Kim's left hand. "By the way, that birthstone ring you're wearing doesn't look much like a wedding set. Before the jet lag wears off of our visitors, Jax needs to do something about that." She whirled away and disappeared from view, intent on making this farce happen.

Kim felt weak. She glanced at her ring, a nice piece of costume jewelry she'd found at a garage sale. She fisted her fingers and pressed her fist to her trembling lips. She was afraid of what she might do if ensconced in the same bedroom with Jax. It was one thing to fantasize about sharing the intimacy of his bed, but entirely another to be faced with the reality.

She shifted to stare at his back. Worried and conflicted, she blinked back tears. The more she stared at him the more conflicted she felt. Jax had a fabulous back. So broad, and such trim, taut hips. Great, muscular thighs, too. She swallowed with difficulty. *Kimberly Norman! Stop that kind of thinking!* She hated the way merely looking at him made her pulse pick up.

She forced herself to look away, but seconds later, his charisma drew her attention. He hadn't moved, still leaned against the counter, his head bowed, looking miserable. Her heart went out to him. Poor Jax. He was as distressed about this idiotic gambit of Tracy's as she.

Kim couldn't understand Tracy's motivation for making up the fake marriage story. Maybe, since Tracy and Jax couldn't fool around this week, she thought it would be funny to make him suffer, force him to spend night and day with Kim.

Clearly the blonde had a very high opinion of her hold on Jax and a very low opinion of Kimberly's sex appeal. Maybe Jax told Tracy he found Kim to be as sexy as dust. Or, possibly, in some bent way, Tracy truly did feel a marriage would be better than a well-meaning-nobody-wife-sitter. Who knew?

For whatever reason Tracy did what she did on her own and it hadn't been Jax's doing. Taking pity on him, she moved close and covered one of his hands with hers. "I'm sorry for shoving you," she said. "I realize it wasn't your fault." She squeezed his fingers affectionately. "I don't blame you."

He glanced at her, and she was stunned by his eyes, glistening with raw sadness. "I'm sorry," he said. "I've never been so sorry." He broke eye contact and stared off. She couldn't tear her gaze from the chiseled angles and shadows of his profile, so sad, yet so dear.

She felt shell-shocked and vulnerable, but decided reassuring Jax was more important than her own self-doubt and pain. "Don't be sad, Jax." Fighting to hold her voice steady, she hugged his middle, resting her cheek against his spine. "We can do this."

She prayed she wasn't lying to herself.

CHAPTER NINE

"I THINK everything went well today," Kimberly said, feeling the agonizing irony of that statement, considering where she was discussing it with Jax. In his bedroom. Nervous, she looked away to focus on the plasma screen TV over the fireplace. "That is—considering…" She couldn't bring herself to say "that we're sharing a bedroom," so she finished weakly, "…our situation."

When he didn't speak, she couldn't help looking at him again. He stood before the wall of windows and glass doors, his back to her, as though he couldn't bear to acknowledge she was there.

"Jax?" she coaxed, feeling awkward and hating the feeling. Jax was her best friend in the world. Just the word marriage between them had already started destroying their closeness. She fought it, refusing to let such an unthinkable thing happen. After all, there was no real marriage.

Hurrying over to him, she took his hand, working to reassure him as well as herself. "Jax, don't be upset. Honestly, nothing has really changed. We're still good friends. This fake marriage stupidity won't alter that." She tried to be cheerful and forced a laugh. "Remember that time we went camping? We shared that tent? You saw me in my underwear and I saw you in yours."

She had been eleven and he'd been fourteen. She'd had no shape whatsoever and her underwear consisted of a T-shirt and baggy cotton panties covered with cartoon figures. His boxers were gray and baggy.

Unfortunately things were different now. Her nightgown was flimsy silk. Luckily she'd packed a long, blowzy T-shirt in case she needed a swimsuit cover. She opted to put that on for modesty's sake so she was only bare from just above her knees down. If she were lucky, he would still wear gray boxers, the bigger and more shapeless the better. Though she'd changed for bed, he hadn't, so she couldn't be sure how hard seeing him in his sleep gear would be. If she were really, *really* lucky he wore full pajamas, top and bottom. She had a bad feeling he didn't.

"And—and this bed is huge," she went on, trying to eke out any positives she could think of about their forced living situation. "A full grown cow could stretch out between us in that thing. And—and besides that, I hardly move at night. You'll never even know I'm there."

She thought she heard him groan. Or was it the wind moaning in the rafters? She checked her watch in the moonlight. "It's eleven o'clock, Jax," she said. "You should think about getting to bed. You said yourself, you and Tracy want to get your promotion going by eight. That means breakfast at seven."

He moved slightly, at least his head did as he shifted to look at her. Without saying a word, he looked away and fixed his gaze on the night sky, the bright moon. He was very upset.

Deep inside, she fought feeling bitter about how obviously upset he was. "Look, Jax," she said, unable to keep her bruised ego totally at bay. "It's not the end of the world, you know. We're adults. We can act like adults. I may not be your bed-mate of choice, but what's done is done. If you want these people as your clients, then deal with it and get over it. What are you afraid of, that I'll attack you?"

He shifted to eye her again. A hollow chuckle, ironic and dark, surprised her. His lip curled in cynical amusement for an instant before his expression grew grave again. "Damn it, Kimberly, just get into bed and shut up."

His harshness caught her so off guard she gasped. Tears welled. Hurt, she reluctantly let go of his hand and padded silently to his bed. A moment later she slipped beneath the covers and presented her back to him. She, too, had a long day tomorrow, the "Mrs." halves of their guests her responsibility for the full eight hour day prior to an outing in Chicago, for dinner and a trip to the theater.

She tried to concentrate on her schedule of activities, but failed miserably. The tears she forced back moments ago, welled again. She let them flow across her face, wetting her luxuriant Egyptian cotton pillow. "Jax," she whispered. "Don't you like me anymore?" Her question was met with a blunt, screaming hush so suffocating she could hardly catch her breath.

Don't I like you anymore? he cried silently. *Don't I breathe anymore? Impossible. I love you, Kim. Can't you see it in every tortured glance? In the way I hold myself, so tense and reserved, whenever you hug me or take my hand? It's not that I don't like you, my love, it's because I want you more than life itself.*

He closed his eyes, gritted his teeth, fighting the urge to run to her, fold her in his arms and beg for her love. He couldn't respond to her whispered query. He couldn't trust his voice.

He cursed himself for barking at her the way he had. Damn his hide, she'd been trying to make him feel more comfortable with an impossible situation that was no more her fault than his. She had insisted they could do this. Sure, *she* could, but he wasn't sure about himself. His bed might be big, but any distance between them wasn't so major that one good roll in her direction wouldn't close the gap.

He stared at the moonlit lake, but all he could see was Kim as she had looked standing there beside him, gripping his hand, working so hard to be his friend. Those eyes, so huge, were lovely, deep pools of compassion. That T-shirt she wore, though oversize, still managed to exhibit moonlit hints of the shapely woman underneath. He grimaced at the stab of desire slashing through him.

Her flowery scent lingered in the air around him, beckoning, teasing, tempting. She had no idea what she did to him simply walking into a room, no idea how the thought of sharing his bed with her tore at his soul.

He feared himself, feared what he might do, even unwittingly, in the middle of the night, half-dreaming, thinking she was yet again a figment of his imaginings. He might reach out, across the small space, take her into his arms, into his dream. He was afraid he might take her body, never knowing, never realizing until too late, that the sharp-clawed vixen in his dream was real, and that he had...

He winced at the emotional blow to his chest. *No,* he told himself. *That's crazy. A man can't—not in his sleep. No rational, sane man could attack a woman and not be aware.*

He was thinking as irrationally as Tracy. Sucking in a long, deep breath, he cleared his head of such contemptible thoughts. He *could* share his bed with Kimberly. And he could do it without touching her. He was a grown man in full control of himself. To suggest otherwise was beneath contempt. He turned away from the window wall and walked into the bathroom to shower and change for bed. A long, frigid shower would do him good.

After toweling dry, he wrapped himself in the white terry, cursing his lack of forethought, not bringing bed clothes into the bathroom. In the darkness, he searched his dresser for something appropriate to wear. Accustomed to sleeping in the nude, this nightwear hunt in inky blackness seemed surreal. What did a man wear to bed for the express purpose of *not* having sex with a woman?

Finally, out of pure frustration and mental exhaustion, he chose a pair of lightweight sweatpants. If he could have stood wearing a sweatshirt, he would have grabbed one. But, even in the winter, he rarely slept with more than a sheet over him. Wearing a sweatshirt to bed would have been like sleeping in hell. Which, he realized with a caustic twist of his lips, was a rather apt description of his current sleeping arrangements— the hell of sleeping with a woman he could never touch.

After returning to the bathroom and changing into the sweatpants, he slipped into bed, careful to keep his back to the woman he loved, so near, yet so tragically far away. He wondered if she was really sleeping, or just pretending, as he would be for the eternity of these next six hours.

The first full day of meetings went smoothly, and Kim was delighted with the way her female charges enjoyed their tour of The Shedd Aquarium, the world's largest indoor aquarium. Kim loved it, too, especially watching divers hand-feed the sharks. Another feature, Animal Encounters, gave them an opportunity to touch a few exotic creatures. Though several of the wives stroked and patted a leopard gecko and an African bullfrog, only Kim got up the courage to touch a Chilean rose tarantula. Nobody opted to caress the red-tailed boa or king snake. Even so, lots of oohs and aahs and giggles were shared.

Funny, but she thought their casual lunch of pizza and burgers in the Bubble Net Food Court, and their visit to Mrs. Field's Cookie House for brownies and coffee were highlights. She had to admit, she enjoyed the chatty atmosphere and breezy conversation over the finger-food desserts and strong, hot coffee.

They spoke of family, children and grandchildren with great affection and pride. Kim hated the lie she'd been forced into living, and the questions directed her way pained her. Luckily, before she and Jax went down to breakfast, they threw together a brief story. Married a month. Honeymooned at their country place, since "we love it so much." Plans for kids? Even though the marriage was a farce, she still blushed at that question. "Oh lots—I hope," was all she said, since the question of children hadn't come up in their story plan.

She self-consciously fingered the wedding set Jax gave her to substitute for her costume ring. It had been the one he bought for the woman he almost married, who had returned it. Kim felt strange wearing a wedding ring meant for another woman. But she supposed that was no more freakish than the marriage sham. In a twisted, backward way, she was fortunate Jax had a wedding set lying around.

She managed to maneuver the conversation away from her "marriage" by suggesting a trip to the gift shop for souvenirs. Much to Kim's relief, that idea was met with enthusiasm. After a half hour of browsing and buying everything from a stuffed toy shark to a sterling angelfish pendent, they piled into the stretch limo, and Mossy drove them home to relax and dress for the evening.

Kim noticed Mossy's attitude toward her had become almost reverent. Poor guy. He actually believed she and Jax had secretly married. It was obvious in his every glance that he wished he were dead for his initial smarmy remark to her when he thought she was a single female employee. It seemed the news of their marriage had been completely swallowed by everybody—well, except maybe Maggie. She didn't question moving Kim's belongings into Jax's bedroom. Still, every so often, she sensed Maggie was dying to ask what was going on, yet the housekeeper was too good an employee to question her employer's bidding. Kim had never been a good liar and felt squirmy, wishing she could explain. But she dared not. If there would be any explaining done, she had to leave it to Jax.

Kim left her charges with a choice of resting in their rooms or enjoying the heated pool for a while before it was time to dress for dinner. As for herself, she opted for the solitude of Jax's bedroom. She was jarred awake from an unscheduled nap on his big bed by the sound of the door closing. She blinked, rubbed her eyes and drew up groggily on one elbow as Jax came into focus. He stood before the door, not moving further into the room. She yawned, covered her mouth, then smiled at him, attempting to ease the tension she could feel every time he entered the bedroom. "Hi." She sat up. "I guess I fell asleep." She checked her watch. "Oh, I'd better get dressed. We leave for dinner in a half hour."

He stood motionless, unsmiling. Maybe it was the fact that she wore her T-shirt. She'd bathed earlier and then slipped into the tee to relax. She'd slept badly the night before, so when she decided to lie on the bed "for a few minutes" she apparently dropped right off into a deep sleep. She ran her hand over her face. "Oh, I haven't put on my makeup." Now she was annoyed with herself. She hopped off the bed. "I'll just grab my makeup kit and get out of the bathroom so you can shower. I can do my makeup out here." She pointed to the dresser mirror. "I won't be in your way."

His brow knit. She couldn't help but notice that darling, sexy dangly curl that forever rode his forehead. "You're not in my way," he said quietly.

She didn't believe him, but wished it were true. "Whatever

you say." She held up a hand. "One second and I'll have my junk out of your way."

"You're not in my way," he repeated.

She dashed into the bathroom and gathered up her makeup, dumping the tubes and brushes into her makeup bag. When she came out, she almost ran into Jax. "Oops." She adroitly sidestepped to avoid a collision. "There, you see?" she said, trying to joke. "I am in your way."

He grunted something she couldn't quite make out as he disappeared into the bath. By the time he finished showering, Kim had her face done. She turned to smile and say "Perfect timing," since it was her turn to retreat into the bath to dress, but her words froze. He stood there wearing nothing but a towel. He met her gaze, shrugged, his expression annoyed. "I keep forgetting to take clothes in with me."

She stared like a starving waif spotting a baked ham as he walked to his closet. She knew her body should be getting up from the chair, should be heading toward the bathroom so she could put on her dress, but her legs weren't cooperating. Whoa, he looked good in a towel.

She licked her lips, gaping as he turned away to go through his suits. He shifted hangers and muscle bulged and flexed in his back and arms. Her gaze drifted down over terry-swathed hips. The towel was damp, so the fabric clung a little too appealingly to those hips. "Naughty towel!" she murmured.

He glanced at her. "Did you say something?"

She swallowed, shook her head. "Uh—no."

He peered at her, his expression questioning. "Aren't you going to dress?"

"Oh—sure." She commanded her legs to straighten and lift her out of that chair.

He turned away but that didn't affect her gaze as it took its tour on down his legs. "Oh—my…" she said, focusing on strong, luscious calves. She must be a calf woman, because those calves turned her on. "Oh, dear…" Her knees felt mushy, but she knew she had a job to do, and that job didn't include gaping at the man, no matter how great his calves were. *And his thighs are pretty fine, too,* some inner gremlin whispered. Annoyed at herself, Kim shoved away from the chair, propelling her sluggish body toward the bathroom. *Change your clothes, idiot!* she coerced inwardly. *Look away from the pretty man!*

Once she managed to get herself into her dress, which hadn't been easy, since her hands trembled from the close encounter with Jax's near nudity, she called out from the bathroom. "Are you decent?"

"Yes," he said.

She came out, checked her watch. "Ten minutes to spare," she said with a smile, then found him. Her smile faltered. He looked so delicious in that dark power suit and red paisley tie. She managed to get to the bed before her knees gave out. *You fool! You fool!* she cried inside. *Don't do this to yourself! He's your friend. Don't lose him by doing anything stupid. Like jumping him and tearing off that suit.*

His gaze followed her as she moved to his bed and sat down hard. "Are you okay?" he asked. "You look flushed."

She made herself smile. "The bathroom was a little warm."

His brow knit. "Oh, sorry. Probably steam from the shower."

Shower steam had nothing to do with her flush, but it was as good an excuse as she might have come up with. Jax, standing there looking so yummy, had everything to do with it. "I imagine." She shrugged, pretending to agree.

A question had nagged her since Tracy pulled this marriage trick on them. She needed an answer. "I don't understand something," she said.

He had shifted around to check his tie in the dresser mirror and was straightening the knot. "What is it?" he asked.

She crossed her legs, hoping to look more casual than she felt. "It's just that—well, I can't understand why Tracy would throw us together—like this. Considering you two are—are so close." That was all she could bring herself to say about their affair.

He turned back, his expression serious. "Tracy is an unusual woman," he said. When he saw her, his expression eased, softened. "You look very nice this evening."

She experienced a thrill at his compliment and her smile became genuine. "Thanks. You look pretty nice yourself."

He half smiled, but only briefly. "Thanks."

As the thrill of his compliment wore off, her smile dimmed. "But, I don't understand why a woman would throw her man into another woman's arms. I mean, well, I suppose she is aware that you and I are just friends, and there's no danger of us—of our—" she held up a hand and wagged it back and forth in an "iffy" gesture "—having...uh..."

"Sex?" he finished for her.

Her cheeks burned. "I—yes. Having—*that*."

He pursed his lips thoughtfully, then shook his head. "There's no telling what goes through her mind. She thought this was a good idea, and being the kind of woman she is, she took it upon herself to make it happen." He walked toward Kim. With every step her pulse quickened. "Tracy is an excellent businesswoman and an indispensable part of my life," he said. "She can read people better than anyone I know." When he came close, he offered her his hand. "Only time will tell if she was right about us."

Kim wasn't surprised by his praise of his partner/lover, but his last comment—only time will tell if she's right about us—confused her. "About us?" She accepted his hand and he drew her to her feet. "You mean about our being just friends?"

"About our being—just friends," he echoed just above a whisper.

"Well, of course she's right about that," Kim said forcefully. Perhaps too forcefully, but it was a truth that needed to be true. "We don't need more time to tell us *that*. Don't you agree?"

He jerked his wrist over to check his watch, his expression closed, as though in concentration. He didn't appear to be listening any longer. "It's time to go," he said, offering her his arm. "Shall we—darling?" he added, without cracking a smile or even glancing her way.

The "darling" took her by surprise until she realized he was getting into character. Obediently she took his arm. "Of course, sweetheart." Though he wasn't watching and couldn't see, she smiled up at him, half wishing they weren't playing a game.

CHAPTER TEN

"WHAT a disaster!" Jax shut the bedroom door between himself, his fake wife and the rest of the world.

Kim winced. "It's not like I don't *know* that," she retorted. "You don't have to growl at me."

"Good Lord, Kim." He glared, his arms outstretched. "Experimental theater? Are you mad? Don't you understand that conservatism and experimental theater are like oil and water? They do *not* mix!"

"But it got rave reviews!" she said.

"Did you actually read any the reviews or just count the damn stars?"

"I read—parts," she hedged. Okay, maybe she went by the stars. "Besides," she added in her defense. "If you'll recall, I didn't have much time. And the girl on the phone at the ticket office recommended it highly."

"I bet she has green hair and is a devout weekend nudist."

"With a title like *Loving Lilly* it sounded perfectly tame. Like a romance."

He shoved a hand through his hair, nostrils flaring. "It was a romance all right, if you think what that horny goat kept trying to do to those poor sheep is romantic."

"That goat's behavior wasn't my fault."

"Who the hell was Lilly anyway? Was there *anybody* named Lilly in that piece of crap?" He yanked the knot of his tie, loosening it. "Except for the humping goat and the bouts of random nudity the plot bored everybody stupid. I heard Mrs. Yoshida snoring. That was before the naked man in jogging shoes ran down the aisle and Mrs. Otaka's screaming woke her up."

"I don't remember any screaming."

"Maybe you're just harder to wake up."

She balled her fists, frustrated. "I was not asleep, and I followed the plot perfectly. I think the jogger embodied society's rush to—"

"Yeah? Well, he needed to embody a pair of pants. The man was flopping around in front of five mature Japanese couples, new to our country, and very likely unaccustomed to seeing either naked joggers or raw goat sex disguised as theater."

"You don't have to shout."

"I'm not shouting."

"Yes, you are!" Her voice broke. "And I don't think you're giving your guests enough credit." Her argument was flimsy, but she couldn't help defending herself. In truth she was horrified about how disgraceful and embarrassing the play had been. But more importantly, she was mortified that she'd let Jax down so badly. Why she couldn't simply come out and say so, she had no idea. Pride, she supposed. It was a flaw, her pride. "Look, I'm good at what I do. But nobody's perfect. So I made a mistake. So you don't get Mr. Otaka's business. It's not the end of the world." She stopped to take a breath and to compose her voice, which had begun to quiver. "I realize you expect perfection, and I'm sorry I didn't live up to your astronomical standards. If you want me to leave, I'll leave. You've made it abundantly clear you don't feel the same way about me that I do about you, anyway."

"What do you mean?" The edge of anger disappeared from his voice.

She swiped at a tear. "Oh, please, Jax. You've been so cool to me ever since I arrived, I'm surprised I don't have frostbite." She sniffed and pulled her lips together to keep them from trembling. He blurred as tears filled her eyes. She whirled away, crushed and shamed, but determined not to let him see her cry. "You've been polite, but you've made it conspicuously clear you don't much like me anymore." Fighting to hold her voice steady, she filled her lungs with air before going on. "Don't bother to deny it."

The room become so still the quiet hurt her ears. "You're being irrational, Kim," he said, finally. "I don't demand perfection, and my feelings for you have never changed."

She sniffed again. "Yes, they have. You don't hug me back when I hug you. You hardly ever smile. You don't tease or kid me. You're so serious all the time I want to scream."

"I've got a lot on my mind."

She made a disgusted sound. "You've always had a lot on your mind, Jax." What did she want him to say? Why had this become a discussion about them?

"This isn't about us," he said, as though reading her thoughts. "This is about tonight."

She whirled back. "Okay, I'm sorry!" she said, her tone as "go to Hades" as anything she'd ever said. "Are you happy now? I made a big, horrible mistake and I should be horsewhipped. I'm very sorry. But I'm even more sorry you're not the same Jax you used to be, because the old Jax would have laughed about this, not gone all ballistic and surly."

"I'm not surly."

"You growled at me." she cried. "Like a—a jackal!"

"Don't be silly."

She flinched at his slight and stood up straighter. "Don't you *dare* call me silly!"

"Look, I have a right to be upset," he said. "That was a rookie mistake."

His bluntness was a slap in the face and she gasped, her pride hemorrhaging. "Rookie?" she echoed in a harsh whisper. "Well, I'm so sorry I'm such an inadequate ignoramus. I'm stupefied that the Crowned Prince Of Precision Decision-Making has put up with a stumblebum like me all these years. You deserve nothing less than *sainthood,* Jax."

"Stop it, Kim," he said, sternly. "I hate sarcasm."

"Oh?" She hiked her chin contemptuously. "The Crowned Prince Of *Precision* Decision-Making hates sarcasm. Well! Off with my head!"

"Stop behaving like a baby," he said. "Hell, Kimberly, everybody in business has to take constructive criticism from time to time."

"Oh, yeah?" she jeered. Vulnerable, exhausted and frustrated, she knew this might not be a great time for rash outbursts, but her hammered pride had taken command of what came out of her mouth. "Well, get *braced* for some corrective criticism from me," she warned with a stony stare. "I *hate* you, Jaxon Gideon. I've never hated anybody more in my entire life than I hate you at this moment." She spun away and ran into the bathroom, slamming the door. He had some nerve.

But you did make a rookie mistake, a voice in her head jeered. *"Oh, buzz off!"* She let the tears flow. "I know it was stupid not to check the play's content, but he didn't have to be so condescending and callous. "I didn't have time to check every detail—and I was doing *him* a favor. 'Loving Lilly' seemed safe enough for—" A sob cut short her defensive monologue. She covered her face with shaky hands and blubbered freely.

She heard a knock at the door. "Kim?" Jax asked, sounding concerned.

"Go away." she cried.

"Are you okay?"

"Don't bother acting like you care now, Jax," she wailed. "It's too late. I'm never speaking to you—*ever* again."

Silence, then, "Fine, if that's the way you want it, be childish."

She started to retort, then closed her mouth. Maybe she was being a little childish. But he hurt her feelings. She couldn't help how she felt, so she'd struck back, giving as destructively as she got. She had a thought and called out, "Tracy thought it was funny."

Nothing. Not a sound.

"Well, she *did*!" She fumbled with the buttons on her suit jacket. What she needed was a long, hot soak in the Jacuzzi bathtub to calm her nerves.

"Congratulations, one person out of twelve of us wasn't outraged."

His gibe galled her. As she planned her barbed answer, she jerked on golden faucet handles. Water began to flow into the sunken, marble tub. "*Two* out of *thirteen*," she shot back, a bald-faced lie. She'd been horrified and disgusted by the fiasco, but the old bugaboo Kimberly Norman Pride wouldn't let her admit it. "Get your facts straight, Jax."

"I thought you weren't speaking to me."

She opened her mouth to fire back, then thought better of it and mashed her lips together.

After a minute, he said, "Very mature."

She gritted her teeth to hold her tongue and finished undressing. If he thought she was going to speak to him now, he would have a long night standing by the bathroom door, waiting, because she would rather kiss a snake.

That same annoying voice inside her head asked, *Are you sure you wouldn't rather be kissing Jax?* She let loose with a low, guttural growl, meant to terrorize the pesky voice in her head. *I can not love Jax that way! Look at what even a fake marriage is doing to us. The decision is made, so shut up about it!*

Too upset to care about her clothes, she tossed them in a heap and stepped into the large tub full of steaming water. She sank down until only her head remained above the surface. Leaning back with an audible sigh, she closed her eyes and worked on blanking everything from her mind—oversexed goats, flabby joggers and cranky-Jax-of-the-oh-so-sensuous-flashing-eyes.

Angry with herself that even furious with Jax and his perfectionism, she couldn't paint him as the villain of the piece. Sucking in a deep breath, she sank beneath the surface. Apparently her head needed a good soaking, too.

Late in the night the water had cooled so much she began to shiver. Either she would have to allow her pride to kill her from hypothermia or she must get out. She'd heard no noise from the bedroom for at least an hour, so Jax had to be asleep. Which was a good thing, since she had slammed into the bathroom without her nightgown.

After drying off, she wrapped herself in a towel that covered all the essentials and crept out to retrieve her T-shirt, in the dresser a million miles away in the darkest corner of the bedroom. Even moonlight streaming through the window-wall didn't penetrate that far. On tiptoe she crept to the dresser and pulled out the drawer with a minimal grating of wood on wood. She held her breath and turned toward the bed to see if the sound had disturbed Jax. Though his face was in shadow, she sensed nothing amiss, like the burning glow of glaring eyes.

Deciding she was safe enough, she slipped the T-shirt over her head, then with a tug beneath her T-shirt, the towel fell to the floor. Now perfectly decent, she scooped up the white terry and padded back to the bathroom to dispose of it in the hamper.

She brushed her teeth and blew dry her hair, frowning at herself in the mirror. What a disagreeable shrew she was tonight. When her hair was dry, she fluffed it, still scowling at herself. Suddenly her reflection blurred; she wasn't surprised. She'd been on the verge of tears most of the time she spent soaking, avoiding the inevitable—an abject apology to Jax.

She might have caused irreparable harm to his and Tracy's efforts to convince these businessmen to hire their firm. "What a self-important jerk you are, Kimberly Norman," she said to her blurry reflection. Plucking a tissue from its bronze holder, she wiped her eyes and blew her nose. After tossing the tissue in the waste can, she flipped off the bathroom light and tiptoed to her side of the bed, slipping beneath the covers.

Unlike the night before, she didn't present her back to Jax, but faced him. His back was to her. Since the bed was situated much closer to the window wall, she could see him clearly, covered from just above the waist with a sheet. His upper body lay exposed. He wore no pajama top, so his strong, moonlit back was hers for all the leisurely viewing she cared to indulge in for as long as she cared to stare.

His spine lay in evocative shadow, a flawless, sinewy trench, curving slightly downward, from shoulders to hips, the long, dreamy length his back. She had a terrible urge to reach across the space and run her fingers along the depression, touch each disk, to know intimately every indention and nub.

She squinted in thought. Did his spine feel like that? Hers did, every bone sharp and palpable. But her back didn't have the marvelous muscle tone his did. Could that much muscle change the texture of a spine? Perhaps rendering it, not only masked by muscle in the moonlight, but armored against detection by touch?

The question gnawed at her. What if she grazed it lightly? Would that wake him? What would she say if it did, that she wanted to know if his spine felt like hers? Pure scientific inquiry should make sense to Jax. It was just a shame that her desire to touch his back had less to do with scientific inquiry than craving physical contact. Touching his back was really a very tiny thing compared to what she wanted—which was a hug and his reassuring promise that they were still best friends. And he didn't hate her for being stupid and silly and childish, not to mention devastating to his business plans.

Her need to touch him, to make a connection, no matter how small, overwhelmed her. She reached out. A scant hairbreadth from her goal, she hesitated. A forlorn tear slid from the corner of her eye to her pillow. She felt so sad, so heartsick and lonely. She refused to deny herself and went with her need.

She touched him, his skin warm against her cool fingertips. When she neither felt nor saw any physical reaction, she grew braver, scooted closer to place the entire palm of her hand against his spine. Yes, she could detect it, though not as distinctly defined as her own. She smiled with the contact, feeling less alone, almost forgiven, though that was a crazy thought. Merely touching Jax's skin didn't give her access to his mind.

Emboldened by her success and the lulling effect skin to skin contact had on her bedeviled emotions, she slowly skimmed her hand from between his shoulder blades down to the small of his back. In order to keep her hand flat against his spine, she slid closer. Moonlight reflected off the wedding set she wore and made the square cut diamond flash like a firefly.

A recollection from her childhood came to mind, when she had been eight, of her joy, catching fireflies in a jar, then dancing around delightedly with her bottle full of sunbeams. She noticed Jax, standing with his bike, watching, smiling, enjoying her pleasure. She remembered running to him and presenting him with her old, chipped mayonnaise jar of flashing bugs, as though it were a king's ransom in jewels. She recalled vividly how, even though he was eleven, and no doubt thought the gift ridiculously babyish, he accepted it with the same solemn ritual with which it had been given.

He even told her he could magically turn the lightning bugs into sunflowers. Sure enough, the next day, he presented her with her own jar, now filled with big, yellow flowers. She had been amazed and thrilled, and wanted to know the magic he used, but he said only, "One day, I'll tell you."

Of course he never needed to explain. She didn't know when she finally admitted to herself that he released the poor bugs out of his back door and replaced them with sunflowers from his mother's garden. She probably knew a year or so later, but didn't admit it to herself for longer than that, simply because she enjoyed the game so much.

That was her Jax. Never laughing at her childish gifts, but giving them special magic. Just being around him held a kind of magic for Kim, so often ignored at home. Jax never showed annoyance or boredom at her immature chattering, which must have, at times, been agonizingly incessant. Her mother constantly complained about her motormouth, but never Jax. Not once.

She spread her fingers, relishing the feel of his skin against her hand. Abandoning the spine, she slid her hand up to the curve of his waist. Blinking back a tear, she whispered, "Jax, you're a big part of my life. Don't be angry with me—please." She loved touching him like this, feeling their connection. She wondered if he would mind waking in the morning to find her so close, her hand reposing on his waist.

"I'm not angry."

Jax's voice startled Kim so badly she jumped. The offending hand flew to her heart. "Oh—I—did I wake you?"

"No." He turned to face her, his expression serious, his eyes glittery and sad. She could see his chest expand as he took a deep breath. "I haven't been asleep."

She experienced a rush of humiliation. "Then why didn't you say something or—or even react when I touched…" She couldn't finish the question and nervously licked her lips, her attention riveted on his eyes, so stunningly forgiving, yet so bleak. He was terribly handsome in the moonlight. Disturbingly so.

He watched her warily, then whispered, "What did you want me to do?"

The question unsettled her. What did she want him to do? She lowered her glance, but could feel his questioning gaze. After a few seconds she looked up, reached out and pressed her hand over his. She couldn't answer his question, but she could try to make amends. "I want to apologize for the way I behaved tonight, Jax," she said. "You were right to be upset, and I deserved your—"

"Don't," he interrupted, taking her hand in his. "I was an ass and I'm sorry."

"No, Jax." She came closer. With her free hand, she caressed his cheek. "Don't apologize. I was wrong." She reached up and wrapped the errant curl around her finger. "And I don't hate you. I'm so sorry for saying that."

"Don't be," he said. "Sometimes I hate myself."

She smiled tremulously. "Well, you shouldn't." She smoothed the curl back into his hair, so soft, like silk. "Jax?" she began, her heart liberated from its awful prison of despondency and alienation. "Would you hug me?" She watched him, full of hope. She knew he forgave her, but would he still be cool to her? Would he comfort her now, when she needed his approval and affection more than she could ever remember in her life? Was he truly the same Jax she loved or a different Jax, a stranger she feared, who only paid lip service to the notion of their close friendship?

She knew they could never be lovers, but she loved him. She couldn't live without his friendship. "Please?" she asked, not wanting to beg, but so in need of his reassurance and validation she could no longer worry over trifles like pride and dignity.

He hesitated only briefly, but she saw it. "Of course," he said, drawing her into the warmth of his embrace.

She inhaled him, loving his scent as she encircled his chest with her arms. "Hug me tight," she whispered, her lips grazing his jaw. He drew her closer and she sighed aloud, clinging with all her might. "You do still care, don't you, Jax?" She tilted her face up to better see him.

He canted his head down. "I do," he murmured, accidentally brushing her mouth with his. The soft contact caused what must have been a static electric shock, only instead of pain, Kim felt a thrill of anticipation, even hope. They stilled, as though dazed. A strange, sweet current pulsed through her, shot along her limbs then ricocheted back to settle deep in her belly where a restless throbbing was born.

For a moment, they shared only the whisper-light contact of their lips. But that soon blossomed into a tender, lingering kiss. Kim had no idea who initiated the intimacy, but initiated it was.

Jax's lips moved over hers in tantalizing exploration, a sensuous enticement for more. She heard herself moan, the wonder of Jax's kiss taking her prisoner, holding her an eager captive. She pressed her body into his, willing the kiss to go on and on. This strange phenomenon that took hold with the brush of their lips was too strong to resist, too powerful to allow judgment or logic to enter into the mix.

Reality faded and Kim found herself in the land of dreams. She felt herself floating, flowing, beautifully mindless as Jax's kiss deepened, his tongue languidly entwining with hers. His hands moved, explored and pleasured. Spellbound with sensations, both familiar and new, she ignored the feeble cry of reason, entreating from some faraway place. She no longer cared. Her world became Jax's lips, his arms, his hands, massaging with a masculine intensity that delighted and aroused her. Husky whimpers of desire escaped her lips, a raw, soulful sound she had never heard before. She trembled with longing.

When their kiss ended, they both gasped for air, their breathing heavy and labored. Nestled against his body, she felt the pumping of his heart. His powerful muscles rippled with tension. The fevered heat of his skin under her fingertips drove her hunger to explosive levels. She moved against him in an erotic body caress, sliding her hand along his back, across his waist to his taut, flat belly. Dipping her hand beneath the sheet, she untied the cord cinching his pants.

"Kim," he murmured hoarsely against her ear. "Are you sure—"

"Shush." She pressed a fingertip against his lips. "Don't talk," she breathed through a sigh. "Just kiss me."

CHAPTER ELEVEN

KIM woke up in a wonderful mood. She opened her eyes with a smile. The first sight she saw was Jax's face, very close to her own as she lay enfolded in his arms. He watched her, his expression tender. "Morning," he said.

Still very groggy, she closed her eyes, snuggled closer and mumbled, "Morning." She laid a hand against his chest, adoring his pleasant, manly texture. She nuzzled his throat, not ready to wake completely. This warm and fuzzy half-dream state suited her fine.

"Sleep well?" he asked against her hair.

She smiled to herself. She'd never felt so rested, so restored, after so little sleep in her life. "Um hum." She sighed. "Shush," she said. "I'm asleep."

She felt his chuckle all through her. "It's nearly six, sweetheart," he said. "We have to get up."

She made a sound in her throat that signaled his news did not suit her one bit.

She felt his hand slide from her waist to pat her intimately on the bottom. "Come on, sleepyhead," he said. "If I can get up after practically no sleep, so can you."

"Mmmm."

He ran his fingers through her hair and kissed her forehead. "What does that mean?"

"Means no." She slipped an arm around him and yawned, cuddling closer.

"Don't do that, sweetheart," he said, his tone tinged with amusement. "Not unless you want me to make love to you again."

She smiled to herself. "Sounds nice."

"Only nice?" he asked. "Last night was much better than nice for me. I must not be very good."

She kissed his collarbone. "You were a very bad boy." Giggling at her joke, she touched him intimately, gratified to hear his groan of desire.

"Kimberly," he said. "Don't do this to me. I have to work."

"No." She ran her tongue along his collarbone. This was a great dream. "Be bad."

She felt him lift her hand away from her erotic manipulations. He kissed her knuckles. "Tonight, my love," he whispered. "Tonight."

She moaned. Must the world intrude on her drowsy little corner of paradise? With a disgruntled groan she rolled to her back and squinted up at the ceiling. The light hurt her eyes. Frowning, she stretched, slowly allowing her mind to swim to the surface, out of the euphoric limbo in which she'd spent the night.

Opening her eyes a little wider, she became more acclimated to the stark light of day. She breathed in deeply, then out, then in again and slowly out. Her thinking processes began to grind into motion. She blinked, frowned slightly as the bare beginnings of full wakefulness took hold. An instant later, her eyes went wide, and she sat bolt upright, nailed by a vivid, beefy flashback of last night and all its implications.

"Oh!" She jerked to stare at Jax, hoping to prove to herself that the images so graphically branded on her brain were a figment of her wild imagination.

Oh, no! There he was, reclining on his side mere inches

away—and not wearing a stitch of clothing—a breathtaking, if disconcerting, sight—Eros, primeval Greek god of passion. *What have I done?* she thought, going into a panic.

"No! No! No!" Grabbing the sheet to cover herself, she scrambled away from him and slipped off the bed. "Oh, Lord—Lord in Heaven...." She held up a halting hand. "This—this *never* happened, Jax." She stared at him with pleading eyes. "This whole night..." She waved in a negating gesture. "Never *ever* happened." She made a broad arc with her arm, indicating the direction of the bathroom. "I'm going to take a shower. When I come out, it's a whole new reality. Do you understand? We didn't..." She swallowed. "I mean, we—we're adults. We can forget about this and—and—and—" she nodded briskly, as though the faster she bobbed her head the easier it would be to make him agree "—and go on as good friends. Right? *Right!*"

He had remained silent as her mood mutated from dreamy contentment into a full-blown anxiety attack, his expression changing from happiness to skepticism. When she finished, waiting for his anticipated, "Right!" he pushed up on one elbow, his gaze not wavering from hers. "Wrong."

His response stunned and frightened her. "What—what do you mean, *wrong?*"

"I mean, no, Kimberly, we can't go on as good friends."

She couldn't breathe very well and she felt dizzy. Planting a hand at her chest, she sucked in several short, panting breaths, working to clear her head, to calm down or at least reduce her level of hysteria. "Come on, Jax," she said, her voice unnaturally high-pitched. "Don't be—don't be...difficult."

"I'm not trying to be difficult." He sat up. "The fact is, things can never be the same between us. And I don't believe you really want them to be." He got off the bed and walked toward her. "Don't be afraid of it, Kimberly. Calm down." He reached for her, but she darted aside.

"I won't calm down!" She scurried in the direction of the bathroom, yanking the sheet hard to detach it from the foot of the bed, so she wouldn't be tethered like a dog on a leash. "There won't be any calming down! Not until you promise!"

Her outburst didn't seem to register on him at all. He continued to watch her solemnly. The morning sunshine illuminated him in such flagrant, sexy detail, Kim felt weak-kneed. Oh, Lord, she'd done exactly what she feared she would do. She'd let her love for him overcome her good sense. She was frightened, petrified. She couldn't lose Jax, she couldn't. Sex was the worst thing she could have allowed herself to do. It always started out fine, but too soon things turned sour. She had to stop this thing before it began—or before it went one inch, er, step further!

She motioned randomly, erratically in his general direction, since there was no way on earth she would actually point. "Please, Jax, put on some pants. You're indecent."

He continued to stare her down. An eyebrow rose slightly. "Don't be a hypocrite, darling." He sounded vaguely angry. "After last night, our bodies are well acquainted." He closed the space between them, grasped her sheet and yanked it away. "I love your body, Kimberly," he said, eyes glittering. "I love looking at you. I love touching you, smelling you, tasting you. I'm insulted you suddenly feel the need to hide yourself from me."

She gasped, stunned, not only by what he said, but by the stormy passion in his voice. She'd never heard him speak with such fervor before.

"Damn it, Kim, after what we shared, I refuse to hide the way I feel any longer." He grasped her shoulders, drawing her against him. "I love you." He kissed her temple, whispering gruffly, "I've loved you all my life. Now that we've made love, I won't lie to accommodate your twisted belief that you must only have relationships with men you can never truly love, never wholly commit to, because of your morbid fear of marriage."

She couldn't allow herself to hear this. She couldn't even let this be happening. Jax could *not* love her. "No, *no*," she cried, pushing against his chest. "This will ruin everything. Having sex was bad enough, but you mustn't love me, Jax. Not—not like that! Don't you see?" She pleaded, "We can't love each other that way. Passion is a double-edged sword. Sure it starts all hot and exciting, but that intensity of intimacy doesn't last. It dulls and dies. Couples fight. They grow to hate each other, and then—then it's over," she finished in a shuddery moan. Tears filled her eyes and she struggled from his embrace to point a damning finger at him. "Don't ever say *that* to me again. I need you in my life, but as my friend. I can't be your lover, Jax. I *won't*. I refuse to love you like that."

He stared, looking shaken, as though she'd shot him with a pistol. An artery throbbed in his neck. For a long moment, he said nothing, then, "I won't be your friend." He made the threat quietly, his voice controlled. "I can't be *just* your friend, Kimberly." He lifted his arms in a questioning gesture. "Why the hell do you think I stayed in Chicago after college?"

She stood mute, too dismayed by his unexpected protestation to think, let alone respond.

"Because..." He clenched and unclenched his jaw. "Because, I decided if I couldn't have you as my wife, I had to get you out of my life." Though his words were measured, his demeanor restrained, she heard raw anger. "I never planned to see you again. But my curse is..." He half smiled, the expression a sham. "My curse is that I love you." His voice caught and he cleared his throat. "You see, no matter how badly I wanted you out of my life, when you appeared, my damn love for you gave me no choice."

She stared, sick at heart, straining to comprehend. Her Jax wanted her out of his life? Had avoided her for years? All this time she thought of him as her best, most loyal friend in the world. She believed him to be the one person who would do anything for her, and for whom she'd do anything. And he wanted her out of his life? It didn't compute. She couldn't make sense of it.

"Have you ever thought about what you'll do to your kids?" His question caught her so by surprise, she stared tongue-tied.

"You don't like the idea of marriage, but you want a man in your life. One day you'll have a kid," he went on. "What happens to the child when you and their father go your separate ways? Then man-number-two shows up, then three and four and so on? You'll be no better than your mother. Worse, because you can't commit enough to marriage because you think of it as the beginning of the end. Good Lord, Kimberly, don't you see, thinking the way you do, you have no choice but to warp another generation of innocent children."

His analysis of her future galled, giving her back her ability to speak. "I don't plan to have children until the right man comes along."

He laughed bitterly. "Why is this so hard for you to get, Kim? There will never be a right man for you. The way you choose men, you've given yourself no shot at permanent happiness."

"You're *so* wrong!" she cried, frantically needing to defend herself. "I only have to find a man I'm completely simpatico with so we never fight."

"And that you have no particular passion for, so you can allow yourself to have children with him?" he added. "And you think that kind of a lukewarm relationship is ideal for bringing children into the world?"

She grimaced, not happy with his characterization of her perfect man. "You're not understanding," she said. "He'll be—of course we'll have passion, because we're so perfect for each other, we'll always agree. Never fight."

He made a disgusted sound. "Look for him in fantasy land, because that's the only place somebody like that exists." The rigid lines of his face broadcast such misery and frustration Kim found it difficult to look at him. She never suspected all these years how badly she'd hurt him. Still, that gave him no right to criticize the way she chose to live. She lifted her chin and met his gaze. "Who are you to tell me I'm wrong to believe what I believe?"

"I'm the man who knows you better than anyone else in the world. The man who loves you."

He was also flawless of face and body, so tall and fit and superbly male. Trying to resist him took its toll, but Jax had a very particular role to play in her life, and that was to be there for her forever as her friend, not a fly-by-night lust-fest who would fade away with the new moon.

If she could only turn back the clock one day. Her world made sense then. It made no sense now. "And—and for your information," she said, trying to reinforce her side of the argument, "until I *do* find Mr. Right—*which I will*—I'm not so stupid or thoughtless that I'd bring unwanted children into the word."

"Famous last words."

His contempt grated. "I won't," she shot back. "Though it's none of your business, Perry and I *never* had unprotected sex."

"I don't give a damn what you and Perry did," he said. "That's ancient history."

She bristled, indignant. "That doesn't change the fact that I'm a stickler—"

"I'm sure you are, Ms. Stickler," he cut in. "Except last night. Unless you're on the pill or taking the shots." He paused for a heartbeat, his remark hanging in the air like a sickly smell. "You do have that covered, right?" he asked.

His question sent a renewed shiver of panic sweeping through her. "Oh—my—heavens…" she whispered. How could she have been so negligent? "Well—it's just that I'm terribly allergic to…" A rush of self-loathing overwhelmed her. "Actually, Perry always…" A second later, she experienced a surge of righteous indignation. This wasn't *all* her fault! How dare he make her shoulder all the guilt. She aimed an accusing finger at his face. "Why didn't you have it covered?" Ugh. Could she have put that any worse? "I—I mean, I wasn't alone in this. You could have been more responsible."

"Remember me? The perfectionist?" His tone mocked her as he threw her faultfinding from last night back in her face. "I'm very responsible, Kimberly," he said. "But last night…"

When he said nothing more, she sensed another boot about to drop, and reluctantly met his gaze. The smoldering flame she saw in his eyes startled and scared her. "Last night—what?"

He scanned her body, up, down, slowly, frankly, and for the first time in some minutes she became aware of her nudity. Feeling vulnerable and insecure, she scooped up the sheet and wrapped it around her. "Last night, what? Damn it!" she demanded, fighting tears.

His gaze traveled over her face, searched her eyes. "Last night," he began, his tone softer, "I thought the greatest miracle in the world would be for you to bear my child." His eyes locked on hers. "I still feel that way." He finished quietly, almost as though in prayer.

She felt herself color fiercely. Jax loved her? Wanted children with her? It was too much! All too much! She shuddered at the enormity of complications today's sunrise brought into her life. Not only had her one true friend told her he would no longer be her friend, he had confessed his lifelong love, the worst possible thing he could have done for her peace of mind. She chewed the inside of her cheek, realizing his admission wasn't the worst thing he could have done.

What if she carried Jax's child?

She loved Jax, yes. That realization was hard enough to deal with, and she was still struggling with it. But she couldn't...they couldn't! It wouldn't work. Everything was unraveling, all the security in her world, dissolving around her. She and Jax only pretended to be married, but they were already fighting. They'd had sex, and though he professed to love her, he would willingly abandon her, trash their friendship, if she refused to see things his way.

A different Jax stood before her today. Ironbound. Overnight, a man she'd loved forever had became someone she feared. Frigid silence surrounded them. Her anguish became a tight knot in her stomach. If she stood there impaled by his dark, brooding gaze for one more minute, she would crumple to the floor in pain.

Desperate and determined to put on a brave front, she gathered the courage of her convictions around her like an impenetrable shield. "I'm going to shower. I don't know about you, but *I* have a busy day planned." Pivoting on her heel, she walked, straight and tall, away from him, hoping running water in the shower would mask her brokenhearted sobs.

The day had been long, but the evening was shaping up to be ceaseless, and not in a good way. Kim planned a catered barbecue on the lawn, with beef ribs, chicken and steaks cooked on the grill, plus corn on the cob, fresh tomatoes, potato salad, fruit and an extravagance of delicious desserts. She also arranged for a party tent with a dance floor, disc jockey and karaoke machine for potential extroverted partygoers.

Dinner at the long, white-clad, outdoor table, ended an eon ago. The dessert table, along with several small round tables with chairs, was set up inside the tent . As the temperature dropped with the aging night, plenty of hot tea and coffee, body warmth and dancing kept the guests from feeling the chill.

Kim checked her watch. Ten-thirty. The DJ was taking his fifth cigarette break, so the karaoke and Mr. Nakamura provided the entertainment and dance music. The sixty-something Tokyo executive stood no taller than Kim's five-six in her bare feet. Wielding an air guitar and belting out "Love Me Tender," the thin, wiry man with snow-white hair and mustache did an enjoyable imitation of a hip-swiveling Elvis.

As miserable as Kim was, she managed a brief, authentic smile—even dancing in her fake husband's arms, their bodies brushing intimately as he pretended to be her doting mate.

"I think Nakamura's good, too," Jax said, surprising her with his perceptiveness.

She grudgingly met his gaze. "How did you know that's what I was smiling about?"

"Educated guess." His grin could charm a bee out of its honey, but Kim could see it for the act it was. His afflicted gaze told a different tale. "I'd be happy to be wrong," he whispered, "and have you tell me your smile was for me, because you love being in my arms as much as I love holding you."

She swallowed with difficulty, her throat parched. "You know how I feel about you, Jax," she said. "I love you. I really do. But according to you, that doesn't count for much—not unless it's on your terms."

She felt him tense, saw his jaw harden. "It's been on your terms for almost thirty years—my love. Don't you think it's my turn?"

She blanched. "But I didn't know that."

"You do now."

He sounded so adamant, so hard. Even smiling down at her as he was, she felt no give, no latitude in his stance. The situation was surreal. Elvis with a Japanese accent crooned in the background. A fake husband with smiling lips and angry eyes insisting she either marry him for real or he would kick her to the curb. "There's no middle ground with you anymore?" she asked, still not able to digest it. "No possibility of compromise?"

"I've compromised all my life, being the friend you ran to when some other man broke your heart. Damn it, Kimberly, it killed me on a regular basis," he said. "I'm through suffering silently. I was stupid to do it for as long as I did. So the deal is, either love me or leave me alone." His smile twisted in self-mockery. "Hell, I've been reduced to spouting sloppy song lyrics."

"The deal is, either love me or leave me alone," she echoed, dreadfully upset, fighting for the life she wanted back. "It may be a sloppy song lyric to you, but to me it proves how little you really care."

He stopped dancing, his smile fading. "Don't give me that bull," he whispered harshly. "Even you don't believe it."

She frowned, disoriented, the world out of kilter. "Don't tell me what I believe."

"Don't lie to yourself and I won't have to."

She coughed, agitated and strangely out of breath. She had to get out of his arms, gain some distance. "Let me go." She tugged at his hold but he wouldn't release her.

His hand at the small of her back pressed her closer. His gaze did not waver from hers, but his eyes changed, grew more heated. "Did I ever tell you how beautiful your hair is in the firelight?" he asked.

She swallowed with difficulty, unable to find her voice. It

seemed that lately every sentence out of his mouth had the power to scramble her senses so badly she could neither think nor respond.

He began to move again, holding her close, their bodies pressed together. He seemed to be purposefully massaging her in just the right way, and just the right place, to arouse and stimulate. He used his body in a manner that was impossible to resist. She could do nothing but flow with him, thrust into him, craving more, ever more, of his potent, erotic contact, unseen by all, yet, oh, so heady and hedonistic.

Never in her life had mere friction between dance partners brought her close to surrender, but Jax's intimate choreography was profoundly clever. The dance became cunning sexual foreplay, and even as distraught as she was, she found herself slipping, relinquishing herself to his will. "Jax," she whispered on a sigh, "that's not fair."

"I don't intend to be fair, darling," he murmured. "Do you realize I know every freckle on your face by heart?" he asked. "Every time I see you I have to fight the urge to kiss them." His body toyed with her, drove her, made her weak.

She closed her eyes and laid her cheek against his chest, all but gone. "Jax," she whimpered. "I'm so confused."

"There's no reason to be. Let me love you, Kim, the way you should be loved. The way you want to be loved." He kissed her temple. "Come with me now."

His soft coaxing drove her wild. Right there on the dance floor, she was losing control. How could that be? They were completely dressed, standing in the middle of a crowd. Desire and need quickly replaced her fear and confusion. She felt his heart beating against her ear and remembered the beauty of that morning as she lay in his embrace. She inhaled his scent, and it, too, brought back passion drenched memories. Her breathing became labored; her pulse rate skyrocketed.

Did she dare go with him? Could she let him do his wonderful sexy magic again, that made her body glow and quake with pleasure and release?

"Darling…" His warm breath titillated. He slipped his tongue into her ear, the lusty contact bringing on a quiver of want. "Say yes," he coaxed. "You want this as much as I do."

She grew increasingly disoriented. Her head spun and she felt faint. Her lips parted with "yes" on the tip of her tongue. At that instant, the disc jockey came on the microphone, loud and jarring, cheerily prodding the audience to give Mr. Nakamura a hand for his performance.

The interruption was like being doused with a bucket of ice water. Kim was thrown rudely back into a bleak, yet saner, reality. She experienced a surge of annoyance at herself for what she almost let Jax talk her into. Her temper flared; she found herself needing to take her near-surrender out on Jax. Brusquely stepping out of his embrace, she faced the DJ and Mr. Nakamura. The Japanese karaoke singer bowed to enthusiastic applause. Kim forced a smile, and joined in the clapping. In an aside to Jax, she said, "Excuse me—*darling*," the last word emphasized for public consumption. "I must speak to the caterer."

That was a lie. But if she didn't get away from him that second, there was a better-than-even chance that the next love song the DJ spun would catapult her over the edge, and she would willingly follow Jax into the night—like a lamb to the slaughter, however earth-shatteringly pleasurable that slaughter might be.

Jax watched her walk away, feeling as though his heart had been cut out. How could he make her see the world of relationships through eyes not blinded by the mistakes of her mother. He was losing hope that the emotional wounds she suffered as a child could be healed. When the applause died and a rousing tune by the Beatles blasted out of the speakers, Jax walked off the dance floor with no particular destination in mind. He was depressed and tired from the day's meetings.

His thought process had been badly corroded, his mind continually drifting away from the important business at hand to his night of lovemaking with Kimberly. Last night had been a night he'd prayed for, dreamed of, for much of his life. How sweetly and beautifully it had begun. Then, as their passions built and played out, the sex—well, it had been surprising—more tender than he could have imagined, almost spiritual. He had never experienced anything so all-consuming, majestic and dazzlingly satisfying, even in his wildest fantasies.

She had to feel it. Deep down, beneath all her resistance and fear, she had to know. They were meant for each other. But how to break through? Was it within his power? He only wished he knew. He would give up all his material successes for the key to make Kim believe that marriage and commitment weren't death sentences to fidelity or passion.

He felt someone take his hand, and hope surged. He turned to find Tracy smiling at him. He hid his disappointment, and smiled at her. "Hey, Jax Man," she said, cheerily. "It's going well, don't you think? I have to give Kim credit. She's done a great job with this picnic idea." She lowered her voice. "The karaoke was brilliant. They're having a ball."

"They seem to be."

Tracy laughed. "After last night's off-off-Broadway screamer, I was afraid we'd lost Yoshida, but he's all smiles tonight. One more karaoke performance by that hilarious man and getting his business will be a slam dunk." She released his hand and grabbed a cup and saucer. "I think I'll have some tea and a decadent dessert."

"You? Allowing noncomplex carbohydrates into your

body? Have you gone mad?" he kidded, working on elevating his mood.

She pushed the lever on the silver hot water urn, filling her cup. "I know you think I'm a saint, but there are times—"

"I've never thought of you as a saint," he cut in. "I've thought of you as a health nut and a workaholic, and quite recently I've come to think of you as a *huge* buttinski pain in the—"

"Oh, hush!" Moving to the tea bag tray, she thumbing through the foil wrapped selections. "My point was, I'm not a saint, which I'm sensing you aren't terribly shocked to hear. Anyway, as far as my being a health nut goes, I do allow myself a dietary indiscretion from time to time."

"Among other kinds."

With a smirk, she peered at him, catching him before he could paste back on his grin. She sobered. "What is it?" She absently swooshed her teabag around in the steamy water. "Weren't you happy with today's meetings? I thought we did great, if I do say so myself." She inhaled, puffing out her chest pridefully. "You were a little off, but I was brilliant."

A little off was putting it mildly. "Yeah, sorry about that. I know I wasn't up to par."

She eyed him critically. "You weren't that bad. I'll even go out on a limb and say you were *semi*-brilliant. Don't be so hard on yourself. We have them eating out of our hands, partner."

He smiled, but only minimally. "I'm glad you think so."

She laid the tea bag on her saucer and sipped the sugarless, creamless brew, her brow creasing in a frown. "You seem down," she said, turning thoughtful. "Can I help?"

He crooked a cynical grin. "Please don't. You've helped enough."

Her thoughtful gaze grew speculative. "Ah." She nodded. "Trouble in the bedroom." Sidling up to him, she whispered,

"Tell all. As your personal buttinski cupid, it's my job to know the very worst."

"And your twisted pleasure."

She looked affronted, though he detected the crinkle of amusement at the corners of her eyes. "I'm insulted. I have only your best interests at heart." She elbowed him. "Come on, give. What happened? Obviously something went wrong. Get any nookie before the roof caved in?"

He didn't like the direction of this conversation so he moved away from her to the coffee urn and poured himself a cup. "Why don't you go be indiscreet with a few mocha mousses and forget about my bedroom."

"The plural of mocha mousse happens to be mocha *mice*," she kidded. "But I digress. Give with the dirt before I have to smack it out of you."

He shook his head and took a drink. "I'm not discussing Kim with you."

She cocked her head, speculative. "Hmmm. That either means nothing happened, or everything did." She pursed her lips in a flitting analysis before concluding, "Since you're bummed, you either feel like less than a man because nothing happened, or guilty that it did."

"Get off it." He inched along the dessert table, scanning the delicacies. "I think I'll eat," he said.

"You're not getting out of this that easily." Her hand hesitated over a crème anglais before moving on to hover above a pumpkin tart. Settling on a gooseberry pastry, fashioned in the shape of a goose, she indicated a nearby table. "Sit with me and talk."

"Not on your life."

She looked put out. "Come on, Jax, I'm dying here. I care about you and I manipulated you and your lady love into the same bedroom for one thing and one thing only. Which was to help you get what's been killing you for way too long—a piece of—"

"Shut up, Trace," he broke in, annoyed. He lost his appetite. He turned away from the desserts and scanned the dance floor. "One of us should be mingling. I'll go. You stay."

"Coward," she said with a taunting smirk. "One way or the other, I'll find out."

He didn't respond, but set his coffee on her table and headed toward Mrs. Inoue. Looking very Jacqueline-Kennedy-retro, Mrs. Inoue wore pearls and a trim blue suit with a short jacket, its sleeves ending just below the elbows. She stood on the sidelines, tapping her foot to the music. She couldn't have made it more obvious she was dying to dance. Her portly husband sat nearby, hunkered over his fourth or fifth dish of rice pudding. So totally was the man engrossed in shoveling pudding into his mouth his poor wife could have been on fire and he wouldn't notice.

Jax supposed dancing with a rice-pudding-widow would be less stressful than being grilled about his sex life by Tracy. He caught Mrs. Inoue's eye, smiling and indicating his intentions with a nod toward the dance floor. She brightened immediately.

The last thing he wanted to do was dance with a near-stranger, making trivial conversation, but he had little choice. He wasn't a child or a bloodied lion. There would be no crawling into a dark cave to lick his wounds.

Face it, Gideon, he counseled inwardly, *You have CEOs to sell and commissions to win. Brooding over Kim might be relentless and agonizing, but millions of people are in pain, and they manage to function. Quit feeling sorry for yourself and play the charming host they expect you to be. You have a job to do. So do it.*

CHAPTER TWELVE

"FANCY meeting you here." Tracy breezed into the kitchen.

Kim sat alone at the large, square butcher-block table, making a few notes to leave for the staff before going to bed. The notes were more of an excuse not to face Jax than absolutely essential. She looked up as Tracy swept in, so tall and self-confident in an amethyst silk nightshirt that showed off a great deal of her long, trim legs. With her matching maribou mules she looked like a tall, vampy sex-siren. Kim felt dowdy by comparison in her navy sweatsuit.

After the party ended over an hour ago, and the guests retired to their rooms, Kim still had last minute work to do, and was dying to get out of her dress and pantyhose, so she showered and changed into the sweats. *At least I'm clean,* she thought dourly.

The blonde grabbed the empty teapot sitting on the industrial size range. "I'm in the mood for a steaming cup of cleansing hot water—how about you?"

Kim couldn't imagine drinking hot water all by itself. "I don't think so."

"Ah, come on." Tracy filled the stainless pot at the copper vegetable sink. "Join me. You'll feel so restored. It's addictive."

Kim shrugged and tore out the page from her notebook to leave on the table. "I guess it can't hurt."

"That's the spirit." Tracy took a seat next to Kim and crossed her long legs as though sitting around half dressed in Jax's kitchen was an everyday event. "Am I interrupting?"

"No." Kim slid the note over for Tracy to see. "Just a couple of breakfast requests from guests. Mrs. Yoshida wants more fresh fruit and Mr. Ishikawa wants miso soup and natto."

Tracy looked interested. "Really? Would the cook have the ingredients for the soup and the other thing?"

Kim shrugged, weary. She'd had a tough day, emotionally, so even idle chatter took its toll. "I looked them up on the Internet, and found out miso soup is made with a paste of mashed soybeans, malted rice, sea tangle—"

"What in Grandma's cupboard is that?"

"I have no idea." She shook her head, bewildered. "I also have no idea what dried bonito and dried sardine fry are, but they're in it, too, plus vegetables, tofu, clams, and seaweeds."

"Hmm." Tracy nodded thoughtfully. "Sounds nutritious. I'd like to try it."

"Maybe you can. According to what I read, instant miso is widely available, so hopefully, by Friday, Mr. Ishikawa can have his miso soup and natto."

"What was natto again?" Tracy asked. The tea kettle began to whistle, so she pushed up from the table.

"It's fermented beans."

"Yum, bean sake for breakfast." Tracy laughed, her mules making a clicking sound on the kitchen tile. "Nothing like getting a snoot full first thing in the morning."

Kim half smiled at the joke. "I think that exact wording is on the label."

Tracy laughed. Grabbing two white mugs from a cabinet, she proceeded to fill them with steaming water. "Hey, you're pretty funny."

"Thanks." The two women had never really talked before. Not that Kim had much desire to. It wasn't that she was jealous of Tracy for her connection to Jax—well, maybe a little. Maybe not. Who knew? Tonight her feelings about almost everything were muddled and out of whack.

Kimberly watched Tracy carry the mugs to the table, dubious about how addictive drinking hot water could be.

Tracy set one mug in front of Kim. "Enough about miso and natto. How are things going for the newlyweds?" She sat, crossed her legs, sipped her water and set the mug down. After a second, she leaned close, startling Kim. "Actually Jax told me about—" she nodded, a look of concerned understanding on her face "—about—you know."

Kim couldn't hide her surprise. The idea of Jax telling anyone about what happened last night had never entered her mind. She felt her cheeks burn and pressed her hands against them. "Oh—dear…"

Tracy touched Kim's arm in a comradely gesture. "It's okay, honey. Jax and I are extremely close. We have no secrets."

Kim supposed she should have known. Unable to sustain eye contact, she shifted to stare at her drink. She suddenly had no stomach to taste it. She toyed with the handle, disquieted. "I guess I shouldn't be surprised. You and Jax being lovers, of course you'd share confidences." She faced Tracy, morbidly curious about her relationship with Jax. "I have to admit I don't understand your thinking, throwing me and Jax into the same bedroom. Weren't you afraid we might—" she halted, embarrassed, and lowered her gaze to her lap "—might do…what we did?"

Tracy said nothing for a moment, then, "You mean, about you two having sex."

She squeezed her eyes shut, as mortified and unsettled as a little girl who'd barged in on something she didn't understand. Shamed beyond words for her horrible lapse, she simply nodded.

"And it wasn't good for you?"

"Oh, no—I mean, yes." She rubbed her eyes, not wanting to say it, but finally admitted, "It was wonderful."

"I see." Tracy's tone seemed more conjectural than crushed. "So, what's the problem? Good sex but zero chemistry?"

Restlessness spiced with a new rush of shame overwhelmed her. "No, there's chemistry. Too much."

"Too much?" Tracy sounded nonplussed.

Kim didn't blame her. How could there be too much chemistry between a man and a woman? "It's just that—I mean for our circumstances." Unable to help herself, Kim faced the blonde. She looked dubious. Before she could voice the expected question, Kim asked a question plaguing her. "Aren't you upset?"

Tracy surprised Kim by grinning as though highly amused. "Why should I be? Jax and I have a relationship with absolutely no fidelity strings attached."

Kim couldn't imagine such a thing. "Really?" She fidgeted with her mug. "I've heard of people being sex buddies, but, well, it seems kind of..." She couldn't come up with the right word.

"Cold-blooded?"

Kim glanced at Tracy. "No. I didn't mean to imply that. It just seems to me that there would naturally be an emotional connection."

"Like the one you felt with Jax?"

"Yes," she said. "I care deeply for him. Don't you?"

Tracy shrugged and sipped her water before responding. "Sure. I'm just not into marriage. At least not right now. Maybe when I'm fifty or sixty, but not now."

Kim exhaled heavily. "Jax told me you didn't want marriage. But I was under the impression he wanted to marry you." She frowned trying to recall his exact words. "He said he wanted to get married."

Tracy nodded. "He does, but not to me."

Kim's mouth dropped open. "You knew?"

She chuckled. "Honey, I've known about you for years." She grasped her arm and squeezed. "And for obvious reasons, I've disliked you intensely." She released Kim. "I can see you're shaken up. You had no idea how Jax felt?"

Kim hid a thick swallow in her throat and turned away. "No," she said. "I mean, I knew he sort of had a crush on me in high school."

"Sort of?" Tracy echoed. "Honey, that's like saying the sun is sort of important in keeping us earthlings warm."

Kim felt humbled and ashamed at being so oblivious to Jax's feelings. But being forced to hear about the depth of his love, and finally understanding how long and how much he'd suffered only made her burden worse. "I don't know what to do."

"Here's one suggestion," Tracy said. "Marry the guy. Put him out of his misery."

Kim covered her face with her hands. "I can't. Marriage kills love."

Tracy chuckled morosely. "You're singing to the choir, babe. Like I said, I'm not into paperwork and long-term intimacy contracts, either, but I'm not Jax. He wants a home and family. Jax and I hadn't been in business together very long when I met his Kimberly clone he *almost* made the mistake of marrying a few years back."

Kim lowered her hands to the table and stared at the wedding set she wore. "Clone?"

"Jax's fiancée couldn't have looked more like you if she were your long lost twin," she said. "Granted, she was a tad taller and she had a prettier nose." She paused. "No offense,

but those upturned jobs like yours annoy the fire out of me."
She went on conversationally, either unaware or unconcerned
about Kim's emotional turmoil. "I like long, swooping noses.
They have pizzazz. No offense, again."

Kim wiped at her eyes with the back of her hands. "She
was really like me?"

"Carbon copy." Tracy tapped her own nose. "Except for that."

Kim grew thoughtful, trying to make sense of everything.
"So you made up that marriage story to throw us together so
we'd have sex?"

"I figured nature would take its course, yes."

Kim frowned, unsettled by how swiftly and successfully
Tracy's manipulations worked. "You thought that by having
sex, Jax and I would fall into a forever relationship?"

Tracy waved off the idea. "God, no. I wanted Jax to get into
your pants so he could *finally* get over you." Apparently Kim's
wide-eyed revulsion at the callousness of the ploy surprised
Tracy. "Oh, are you offended?" she asked, clearly more inquisitive than troubled. "Sorry. But you've got to remember, that
Jax is my partner and the dearest friend in the world. And you..."
She paused, casually shrugging again. "Remember, I hated you
for years, hardly know you now, so I didn't care how you felt."

Kim gaped, unnerved. Her temper veered sharply toward
anger. "Well, in case you're curious, I'm upset. My world is
crumbling. Are you happy?"

Tracy's forehead furrowed. "Aw, you're mad."

How could she even pretend surprise? "Wouldn't you be?"

Tracy lifted her mug, took a sip, appearing to think it over.
When she set down the drink she canted her head as though
still considering. "Now let's see. If you maneuvered me into
bed with Jax?" She grinned. "Without going into colorful detail, I'll just say our situations are vastly different. I wouldn't
be mad, though."

Right, as Jax's noncommitted sex buddy, why should she be mad? Not a good example. "I can't imagine why you find this so funny," Kim said. "What you did was horrible."

"I don't think it's funny." She eyed the ceiling then, shaking her head, she planted the flat of one hand on the tabletop in a jarring slap. "Okay, you got me. It's a little funny."

"Well, excuse me if I don't laugh, but exploiting people like they're your own little puppet show is *not* amusing. As a matter of fact, it's despicable!" Kim had never felt so exploited and deceived. She pushed up to stand; her chair almost pitched backward in the flurry of her liftoff. "If you want my honest opinion, I think *you're* despicable!"

Tracy raised her mug in a cheery salute. "*Que sera, sera,* baby."

Dumbfounded by the blonde's nonchalance, Kim gasped. "How can you sit there so bloodlessly cool? You should be ashamed!"

"Should I?" Tracy inquired. "Then answer me this, Kim. If the situation were reversed, and you were Jax's partner, and you watched him suffer over fickle, self-absorbed me for your *entire* friendship, and you thought maneuvering us into bed would help him get over me, just what would you have done differently?"

Fickle and self-absorbed? Is that how people saw her? Is it how Jax saw her? Had he discussed her in those terms with Tracy? Her heart lurched at the very idea. When she tried to speak her voice wavered. She cleared her throat and tried again. "But I would do anything for Jax."

"And I did what I did—*for Jax,*" Tracy said, losing all humor. "It pains me to see him unhappy right now, but at least now that he's been able to burn off some of his pent-up lust for you, he can begin to put your thoughtless, fickle self behind him and move on."

Thoughtless? Fickle? "But—but I'm not—I never meant to be those awful things. When Jax was my neighbor, as a kid, and he had troubles, he could come to me. He could have done the same thing any time in these last ten years."

"But he didn't, did he?" Tracy reminded.

Kim experienced a sharp stab of regret. Why had she never sensed any of this? "But he could have," she cried. "I would do anything for Jax. Anything!" she said, parroting the life-long refrain. "He's the one solid thing in my world, and I can't lose that. If we became lovers, I would, don't you see? That's why I can't be his lover or his wife. But as his friend, his *best* friend, I'd go to the ends of the earth for him."

"You'd go to the ends of the earth, all right," Tracy said, her tone contemptuous, "to disturb him with your problems at the drop of a hat, no matter how intrusive. With a best friend albatross like you hanging onto him, Jax doesn't need a meddling, whiny neighbor. You know the type. She'd barge in uninvited, hang around boring the pants off of him—no pun intended—then foist herself on him for dinner, maybe break-fast, whatever. Finally, when she's filled up with food and self-confidence again, she struts off, ignoring him until her next personal crisis." She hiked her eyebrows, challenging, "Sound familiar?"

"That's not fair," Kim said, uneasy with Tracy's descrip-tion. She was afraid there might be a grain of truth in it. "I love Jax. If I ever thought I was bothering him…" She became more uncomfortable by the minute, her dismay billowing. "I would never knowingly give him one bad moment. Not one second of sadness. I'd cut off an arm first," she swore. "How many times do I have to repeat it? I'm his best—"

"No, Kimberly," Tracy interrupted. "*I'm* his best friend. You're the woman he wants to forget." She stood up to tower over Kimberly, her expression stern. "I'm sick of seeing him hurting because of you, and I'm thrilled he seduced you. I'm not sorry for helping him do it." She lifted her mug and slugged down the rest of the water. "Ah, that hit the spot." She eyed Kim, a corner of her mouth lifting in a caustic smirk. "So you two had sex. So what? It's not like you were saving yourself for marriage. And since you have no intention of committing matrimony with him or, most likely, anybody, take my advice. After this week's meetings are over on Saturday, get the heck out of Dodge. If you get my drift." She indicated Kim's hot water. "Are you going to drink that?"

Devastation and anger choked off Kim's ability to speak.

"Mind if I take it?" Without waiting for an answer, Tracy plucked the mug off the table. "Thanks. Well, night, night, sugar." The blonde winked, spun away and headed out the door. "Sweet dreams."

Ravaged by sadness and numb with rage. Kim could do nothing more than stare after her.

Jax had no intention of going to bed before Kim returned to their bedroom. He knew she was avoiding being alone with him, but he was a patient man. He intended to have a talk with her, to convince her that marriage could be a loving, lasting bond, if the two people entering into it cared enough to be sensitive, open, honest and willing to do the work it took to keep things fresh. They had to want to be aware and receptive to the other's needs. The problem with Kim's mother had been selfishness, laziness and the idea that white-hot passion was the only valid expression of love.

Her big mistake was to *not* realize love could be soft and full of subtleties, like the simple joy that brought a room to life whenever the one special one walked in, or her scent lingering in a closet that brings on a smile, or the anticipation of her groggy good morning kiss.

Kim's mother had the foolish, destructive notion that once the initial thrill faded, love ended. So she quit prizing her partners for the individuals they were and she grew bored. Her boredom bred dissatisfaction, which led to exasperation, frustration and anger. Ultimately Kim witnessed the inevitable fights and ugly splits. Not once, but again and again.

Insensitivity, selfishness and laziness killed off relationships, not the ceremonies or the sex. "But how do I convince you of that, Kim?" he mumbled. Hunkered on the edge of the bed, his forearms resting on his thighs, he focused on the beige carpeting, seeing nothing in his mind's eye but Kim's stricken face. Brutal, helpless bitterness slashed through him. His thoughts tasted like gall. "How do I breach a wall forged from a lifetime of toxic object lessons?"

He heard the door and his head snapped up as Kim entered. She paused, as though startled to see the room bathed in light, her fake husband, in low-riding sweatpants, still awake and staring at her from across the room. After a second's hesitation, she regained herself and closed the door at her back. "Hello," she said, her expression clearly meant to mask any emotion she might be feeling.

"Hi." He straightened. "All done?"

She nodded, avoiding direct eye contact. "I thought you'd be asleep."

"No," he said. "We have a lot to talk about."

She flicked her gaze at him, then seemed to remember she didn't want direct eye contact. She quickly shifted her attention away. "I don't think so, Jax." She walked to the dresser on the far bedroom wall and fished out her sleeping T-shirt. "I'm tired. I just want to sleep."

Her composed declaration tore at his gut. She just wanted to sleep. He wanted to hold her, love her, commit himself to her, body and soul, for the rest of his life. If he allowed him-

self to think about it, the utter polarity of their wants was gro-
tesquely funny. He chuckled deep in his throat, the irony making him so miserable it was either laugh or cry.

Apparently Kim heard, for she turned abruptly to face him,
her sleeping tee clutched to her breast. "I'm getting sick of
being laughed at."

Puzzled, he stared at her. "What?"

"Oh, like you don't know." She walked toward him, scowling him down.

He watched her without comment.

"I should have known you would find last night's seduc-
tion too titillating not to share with your sex buddy."

"My—*who?*"

"Oh, please! Don't deny it," she said, her tone scoffing.
"We just had a chat in the kitchen, and she told me everything."

"Who did? You and Tracy?"

"How'd you guess?" She reached him and shoved at his
shoulders. "You two pulled off the perfect con so you could
seduce me to forget me. Nice job, Jax!"

He frowned at her twisted recollection of the facts. "*I* seduced *you?*" he asked, incredulous. "How, by being awake?"

"You were a damn sight more than awake, my friend!" She
poked his chest. "You were lying there…" she poked again
"*planning* your strategy of attack." She poked once more,
then left her hand on him, pressing her fingertips against his
chest in a stiff-armed, multipronged jab. "You know it."

"There you go, touching me again." He grasped her wrist
gently. "Do you realize it's always you who initiates physical contact?" As he spoke, he tugged her closer, pulling her
wrist down and toward his waist until she not only stood between his legs, but her breath grazed his face. "I wonder why
that is?" he whispered, stealthily sliding his free hand to her
waist, his fingers breaching the band of her sweatshirt. A sec-

ond later he skimmed his hand against her bare waist, then up along her ribcage. The warm contact tingled his palm.

Kim's knees buckled, but his quick reflexes landed her on his lap instead of the floor. He watched her face, watched the curve of her mouth change from a frown, softening into pliant, half-opened lips. Her narrowed eyes, the irises pinpoints of darkness, grew wide, luminous, and darkened as her pupils dilated. She shivered almost imperceptibly. Her lashes fluttered down as his hand ascended to cup a full, sweet breast.

"No bra?" he inquired, his voice already rough with arousal. Damn him, this wasn't the rational conversation he planned. But with her hips teasing his groin, her naked breasts intensifying his hunger, her lips slightly open and welcoming, and—blast him—if that mouth was not pleading that he make love to her, he never knew her at all. And he knew her, better than he knew anyone else. "Did you have something more to say, darling?" He teased her lips with his, nipping at them lovingly.

"I—I can't...remember..." she whispered.

She said nothing more, though her lips remained invitingly parted. He accepted her invitation, slipping his tongue inside her mouth. She moaned her pleasure. When he released her wrist, he delighted in the way she clung to him, her nails biting into his back. "Jax," she sighed. "Oh, Jax...love me!"

"I always have," he murmured. Tumbling to the bed, he pulled her down with him. She lay on top, her kisses, urgent and charged with desire. Fire raged through every nerve in his body. He cupped her bottom, pressing her into him. A feral sound came from her throat. Their tongues darted and danced with a driving, pulsating need. She clung to him, moved against him, fanning the flames. Her ardor was primitive, exciting. Beautiful.

She reached down to caress him and he cried out in pure,

gasping passion. He felt such unspeakable longing, such unquenchable adoration for this woman, so intense, inspiring, yet sweetly gratifying in surrender. He always knew he loved her, but never realized how deep and wide and boundless the feeling could be, never having experienced the earthy, wild Kimberly he discovered last night.

The revelation had been as shocking as it was thrilling. Now that he knew her so intimately, his life would never be the same. His understanding of what it meant to be fully alive, to be truly loved and in love, had been forever transformed, exalted. If he lost this facet of Kimberly, it would be like losing his eyes and his mind.

When this week ended—if she decided to turn her back and walk away—Lord, help him.

CHAPTER THIRTEEN

ON THURSDAY morning when Kim woke up she knew exactly where she was, and in whose arms she lay. Jax was asleep, so she had plenty of time to gaze at his face in repose. Long, dark lashes fanned out across prominent cheekbones. His lips curved slightly upward at the corners, as though his dreams held only pleasant images.

Her lips trembled as she smiled in tender homage to the quiet, kind neighbor boy who had grown into a handsome, giving man, her close friend and confidant for most of her life. The man to whom she'd always turned when her heart was broken, an act she now knew had been a great burden to him, but one he bore with dignity and in silence.

She pressed her lips against his jaw, unable to help herself. "I've hurt you so, Jax," she whispered. "I'll never forgive myself." A tear slid across her cheek to his shoulder.

Her melancholy mood encompassed more guilts than that one, though it was paramount. Another sorrow she harbored was the knowledge that tonight she would once again fall helplessly into his arms. She knew this as surely as she knew the sun would set on yet another crisp October day. For she had found in Jax a gifted lover. He made her body feel things she didn't know were possible to feel. He could take her to heights so heady, so intoxicating, she feared becoming addicted.

In the clear light of dawn, she now had to face her third, most conflicting regret. She must find the courage to leave Jax while they were both still reeling with desire, while new love's fire glowed in their eyes, heated their bellies and drove them to the frenzied lovemaking all new lovers shared.

She had to be strong, resist the urge to be fainthearted. She closed her eyes, unwilling yet to leave the solace of his embrace to face twelve long hours away from this man, whose lovemaking was both breathlessly gentle and exhilaratingly bold. She blushed, experiencing a rush of heat in the deepest part of her as she relived, in her mind, the blissful texture of his belly, hard against hers, as he drove himself into her, again and again. How clearly she recalled crying out, glorying in his virile mastery. Wild magic was alive in his body, his kisses, so wild and magical their potency hurtled her up, up, until she abandoned herself in gasping tremors of ecstasy.

Yes, she loved Jax as she'd never loved any man—much too much to allow their relationship to become ugly. That was precisely the reason she had to dig deep within herself, find a reservoir of strength to sustain her. So that now, this very moment, she could start storing up courage to keep focused on her goal, two days away. On Saturday, long before frustration, anger and nastiness could begin to erode their happiness, she would walk away from Jax.

Forever.

When he and Tracy returned from the airport after seeing off their guests, she would be gone. Leaving without even a goodbye might seem cowardly, but she didn't believe a drawn-out parting would benefit either of them. And from what she'd recently and vividly discovered about Jax's sensual power, if they touched, even if he took her hand, she would be lost. She would be his and she would stay. They would make promises to each other that one day they would break.

No. Though creeping away behind his back might seem sniveling, even cruel, she knew in her heart that it was the kindest, least painful choice for them both.

She caressed his cheek, her hand tingling with the bristly texture. Even such a small thing turned her to mush. If he were awake, all it would take was his grin, and she would once again give herself to him gladly and fully.

Before anything so dangerous happened, she rolled from his embrace and out of their bed, padding to the bathroom. Before her loomed another day of acting the cheerful hostess, smiling on the surface, while underneath, her heart finally, *genuinely* broke apart.

How ironic that, this time, she would have nobody to run to.

"Hey, Jax Man." Tracy grabbed him around the waist and squeezed affectionately. "You're so chipper today. I'm a little surprised." They milled with hundreds of other Chicagoans at Kimberly's final group outing, an Art Walk and street fair. Being Friday, the final day, Jax and Tracy ended the business meeting after their morning session, to include the husbands in their afternoon outing.

Their Japanese guests were on their own for the next couple of hours, to enjoy the informal opportunity to view art, speak unhurriedly with artists from local studios, as well as visit interesting eateries, churches and open spaces where swing and jazz concerts made fun, energetic entertainment.

Jax grinned at Tracy. "Why shouldn't I be in a good mood?" If the truth be told, he'd never been happier. He didn't even care if they got any business from this week's work. All he knew was that Kim had been very willing to spend her nights making wild, wonderful love with him. He could hardly believe his luck. He wrapped an arm about Tracy's shoulder. "I'm a happy man."

Tracy's expression exhibited doubt. "No kiddin'? I guess I figured after I gave Kim the straight skinny on why I got you two together, she'd be angry at you."

"She was for about five minutes, but…" His mind tripped back to how quickly and completely she'd melted in his arms. "She got over it."

Tracy smirked. "Holy cripes, Jax Man, what have you got, anyway, some kind of magic wand?" She grimaced. "Considering you're a man, maybe that wasn't the best word choice, but, I'm starting to think the rumors about you are true."

He didn't enjoy Tracy's jokes about him having some kind of legendary sexual prowess, and frowned. "Cut the crap, Trace. It's just that she and I…" He shut his mouth, then said, "We're not going to discuss this. Let's just say Kimberly and I are getting along fine."

Tracy shook her head, as though baffled. "I'm impressed. Even after she found out you were getting in her pants to get over her, she still willingly committed hanky-panky with you."

"That's putting it pretty crudely," he said. "And not true."

Tracy rolled her eyes. "What do you mean? It was the plan."

"Not mine."

She looked more closely at him, as though attempting to read his mind. "You're not saying you think this thing is permanent, are you?"

He couldn't be upset today, and smiled. "Don't be such a pessimist. She loves me. She said so."

"Oh—holy—*hell*," Tracy said. "You dreamer!" She looked away as though dying to yell her head off at him, but considering where they were, struggling to curb her tongue. When she faced him again, her expression was pinched, exasperated.

"Oh, come on." She motioned toward a small gallery, its name painted on the door in a garish psychedelic design, The Gnu Niche. "I've heard excellent things about this artist and I'm looking for a piece that speaks to me to go in my entry hall." She grabbed his arm and pulled him inside the enclosure, crammed with scrambled expressionist abstracts, raw cubism, three-dimensional reliefs and a few freestanding sculptures.

Jax wanted to find Kim, wanted to be with her, simply hold her hand, but he allowed himself to be drawn inside. The last time he'd seen Kim she was working, finalizing the dinner menu for their party at one of the picturesque local cafés that boasted a Bohemian keyboardist, a cult favorite, who played a 1930s era harmonium, or reed organ.

"What do you want this art piece to say?" he asked. "Hi, I'm an annoying wet blanket?"

She frowned her disapproval at his description. "You're so funny, but no. I'd like a sculpture. If we could find something like Auguste Jean-Baptiste Clesinger's 'Woman Bitten by a Snake,' but sexier, I'd be really happy."

Jax eyed her critically. "So you want this sculpture to say, 'Hi, kiss me, I'm poisonous?'"

"Shut up. You're hopeless when it comes to art."

"Then let go of my arm. I want to find Kim."

"No. Forget about her and help."

He scanned the studio absently, seeing nothing that interested him. Hell, he was a man deliriously in love. Nothing else mattered. "I can't forget about her."

She dragged him in her wake. "Look at this," she cried, excitedly.

Jax turned to see a large pigeon constructed from hundreds of children's books.

"Isn't it fabulous?" She threw a hand to her heart, as though awestruck.

He squinted at it to see if it looked any better with his eyes nearly shut. "It's not speaking to me."

She released him and rounded it, examining it with a critical eye. Jax watched her, amused. "I feel I must tell you something about pigeons that you may not like."

She peered at him. "I happen to love pigeons. What could you possibly say that would bother me?"

"They're monogamous," he said. "I'm afraid they mate for life."

She made a pained face. "Okay, you can stop helping now, Mr. Wet Blanket."

He grinned. "One good wet blanket deserves another."

Tracy ignored him and called over the proprietor, apparently still interested in the monstrous bird, even with its diametrically opposing view of commitment to her own.

"Have fun," he called over the drone of meandering visitors.

Without looking in his direction, Tracy impatiently waved him off.

Now to find Kimberly. He smiled to himself, feeling relaxed and invincible. His life had become something wonderful, almost beyond belief. The air smelled fresher, food tasted better. He could laugh at anything. Sometimes he laughed at nothing at all. It seemed criminal to be so cheerful, to finally feel whole and alive.

Two weeks ago, he would never have believed how swiftly all his dreams could come true.

CHAPTER FOURTEEN

KIM stepped inside Jax's bedroom and closed the door. She leaned against the wall, conscious of a dull throb of grief in her chest. She stood there, alone, amid the ashes of Jax's friendship, for so many years her safe harbor from the storms of life.

Only a moment ago she said goodbye to him, to Tracy and to the five Japanese couples she'd grown fond of this past week. Jax kissed her goodbye, as a loving husband might. She could still taste his gentle passion. He hadn't been playacting. He loved her. He'd lived that love all his life, in word and deed. And over the past few, precious nights, he'd physically proved the depth of his love with breathless artistry. Her pulsebeat escalated at the mere thought.

She closed her eyes. "Oh, Jax," she whispered, her voice quivery and forlorn. "I wish—" What did she wish? That she could stay and be his lover for as long as it lasted? Or perhaps that they'd never had sex? That she could walk away clean, without the knowledge that under Jax's tender tutelage her body had experienced the thrill of soaring far above the earth?

Which did she wish? *Maybe you wish that you and Jax could go on as friends and lovers for the rest of your lives,* a little voice niggled. *That you could legitimately wear his wed-*

ding ring, bear his children. Be in a solid, lasting relationship. Have a whole, caring, loving family.

She wished so many things, some so dead opposite, she couldn't fathom which ones she wished for the most. "Probably the fantasy—the 'happily ever after' cliché." She shook her head. "Yeah, and how many times does that happen?" she grumbled. With the divorce rate growing like the kudzu weed, chances were better than even that they would end up calling names and throwing lamps, leaving horrible emotional scars.

"No, Jax." She swiped at a tear. "I refuse to let us end badly." Her voice broke. "I'm ending it while we're happy." She straightened, good intentions spurring her on. Trying not to think, she slipped off the wedding set, walked stiffly, determinedly, to his bedside table and laid it down. For a long moment she could only stand there, staring at it. She had always hated marriage, seeing it as a grim, gray sort of merging, too easily burst apart. Oh, the trappings were pleasant enough, the white gown, the glittering diamond. But in the end, they were nothing more substantial than frothy icing masking a bitter cake.

"So, get moving, idiot!" she said. "Stop staring so longingly at one of the major booby traps. You know it for what it is. Get packed. Be on your way before Jax returns from the airport." She bent down, opened the top drawer in Jax's bedside table and swept the rings inside. "You've been pumping yourself up for this moment for days." She slammed the drawer shut. "The time has come to quit sniveling and do it." Her resolve stiffened, she grabbed the bedside phone and called Maggie's extension. The housekeeper answered. "Yes, Ms. Kimberly?"

Kim took a second to gather her poise, then said, "I need a taxi as soon as possible. I'm leaving. And I'd appreciate some help packing."

The overlong pause didn't surprise her. She knew Maggie must be floored by the news. The tender way she and Jax behaved with each other these past few days didn't go unnoticed among the staff. More than once Kim glimpsed real pleasure in Maggie's eyes, as though she believed her boss had finally found true happiness. It pained Kim to hurt him, but she knew in the long run, she was doing them both a kindness.

"I'll be right up."

Though Kim sensed Maggie wouldn't pry, she knew she wouldn't be able to handle the housekeeper's probing gaze. "I would rather you send one of the maids, please, Maggie," she said as calmly as she could. "Just call a cab for me."

"I—yes, certainly."

Kim hung up, felt a sob rising in her throat and covered her mouth to strangle it. *Get hold of yourself,* she warned. *Do not cry! Get your suitcase out of the closet and start packing.*

When she heard a light tapping at the door, she had already opened her bag on the bed and begun to pull lingerie from her dresser. "Come in." She glanced up to see one of the temporary staff standing there. "Please take the things out of here and pack them. Then add the dresses in the closet. I have to…" She hesitated. *I have to go into the bathroom and cry,* was the truth, but not what she intended to say. "Do—something…" She waved vaguely toward the bathroom. "When you're done, ask Maggie to ring me when the cab arrives."

"Yes, ma'am," the plain young woman said with a smile. "My pleasure. And may I say, it's been a joy working for you and Mr. Gideon. When you need extra staff again, please ask for me in person. Sara May Pottorf."

A wave of depression washed over Kim at the knowledge that the need, at least with her as hostess, would never happen. "I—sure," she lied, afraid of bursting out sobbing in front of the poor, clueless woman. "Excuse me." She escaped to the refuge of the bath.

Once inside, she dropped to the edge of the marble tub, emotionally wrecked. Blinded by tears, she fumbled with the bathtub handles, eventually managing to crank on the water full blast. Her shoulders drooping with despair, she pressed her forehead against the chilly marble wall and let soul-deep sobs flow, in a way mourning her own death.

Jax returned alone, since Tracy wanted to be dropped off at her Chicago loft. He strode inside, a man in total command of his world. He felt like a long distance runner hitting his stride. The world was a wonderful place, and today was a fantastic day to be alive.

This week had been the best of his life, and he wasn't even thinking about the business meetings. He couldn't care less about that, though he already had assurances from Ishikawa, Yoshida, and Nakamura that they would utilize Gideon and Ross's services.

As far as he was concerned, if any of them wanted consultations between now and the new year, they would be dealing with Tracy alone, because he planned an extended honeymoon in the Bahamas. Or Europe. Hell, he didn't care. He would be happy to spend his honeymoon in a cramped, cold-water flat if Kim was there. But, luckily, he could do a damn sight better than that, and he intended to. All Kim had to do was name the destination, and after an intimate ceremony, they would disappear into their own newlywed paradise.

He saw Maggie approaching along the hallway that lead from the kitchen and grinned, offering a jaunty salute. "We did good, Mag," he said. "Tell the staff there will be a twenty-percent bonus all around. Where's Kim?"

Maggie's serious expression didn't seem appropriate for such good news. He experienced a prick of unease. "Is something wrong?"

Maggie came to a halt at the cusp of the entry hall, her hands clasped before her, her head slightly downcast, as though harboring a guilty secret she knew she could no longer keep.

"Maggie?" All sorts of scenarios rushed thorough his mind. Had the cook made off with the sterling? Who cared? And so what if some maid spilled a whole pitcher of grape juice on the living room's snowy wool Berber? He was too happy to worry about *things*. Things could be replaced. "I'm sure it can't be that bad."

She swallowed, looking distressed. His usually confident, upbeat housekeeper made an intriguing, unsettling sight. He'd never seen her lose her composure, and looking at her now, she seemed on the verge of tears. He walked to her, prepared to comfort her. "What is it? Is it your husband? Is he okay? The kids?"

She shook her head. "It's Ms. Kim."

His heart lurched with alarm. He grasped the top of her arms, panic grabbing him by the throat. "What happened? Is she hurt?" The visions whipped in furiously, terrible scripts, his worst nightmares. A tumble from the balcony? A fall down the stairs? A bathtub slip and drowning? Or some cruel act of God, like a brain aneurysm, stealing her from him on the brink of their lives together? From Maggie's face he knew it had to be bad. *"Lord!"* His grip tightened. "Tell me! What hospital?"

Gesturing toward the door, Maggie said, "She's gone. She said to tell you not to—not to go after her. I'm sorry," she said, her voice a hoarse croak. "I'm so—so very sorry."

Jax's grip on her tightened, his mind closing down, blocking what she told him from his consciousness. He grimaced at an odd ringing in his ears. "There, there." He murmured, his mind clouded. His brain took in only short bursts of gar-bled images. He knew he should search for the meaning of Maggie's words, but a stab of foreboding made him resist—a whispered warning rang across his rational blackout—that to understand her words would bring with it unbearable pain. "It's okay," he heard himself say. He felt like he was some-where outside his body, looking down. "Everything's—all right."

"Oh, Jax…" she said. "I never thought she could be so hateful and spineless. I don't know what to say."

He thought he felt a quick kiss on his jaw. He frowned, con-fused, blinked, rubbed his eyes. After a moment, when he looked around. Maggie was gone.

Slowly, slowly, he allowed himself to begin to absorb what she said about Kim. It was hard work, thinking, fathoming, gradually allowing himself feel the full onrush of pain. Kim had gone away, without even a goodbye. He burned with love for her, and she never wanted to see him again. Memories closed around him, filling him with a longing to turn back time, cast off this pain of the damned. But, no. Even he, with all his wealth and power, could not pull himself out of this dark place, to gain again the naïve bliss that was yesterday.

Focusing on the staircase, he walked toward it, numb. Halt-ingly he moved up the stairs, aware only of a suspension in time and space, of falling, tumbling out of control, in an emp-tiness so vast, silent and cold, neither light nor warmth could find him.

CHAPTER FIFTEEN

KIM sat alone in her apartment in front of a cold, empty hearth, watching a sitcom rerun. She poked at her tasteless microwave dinner of turkey and dressing, green beans, yams and a red, glutinous matter that the dinner box blithely referred to as cranberry sauce. She picked at the red goo with her fork. "If this gunk ever even passed through a state with a real cranberry farm, I'm—" She stopped short. She'd almost said, "I'm having a happy Thanksgiving." Which she wasn't, but why grouse out loud?

"So you're alone." She stabbed at the goo. "So what? Lots of people are alone on Thanksgiving and they're perfectly fine. I'm perfectly fine, too."

She picked up the TV remote that shared the TV tray with her cardboard dinner plate, and switched to some traditional rah-rah Thanksgiving football rivalry. She stared at the running, chasing, tumbling mass of professional athletes. "Football is a Thanksgiving tradition," she reminded herself. "It's what we do on Thanksgiving. So what if I don't enjoy the game? I will watch it and cheer for—somebody."

After a few more confusing minutes of watching men in blue and silver ram themselves into men in red and white, she flipped off the TV. With a weary sigh, she tossed the remote to her pink chenille sofa, one of the several pink chenille pieces she rented after her mad dash home from Chicago six weeks ago. After all, she couldn't live in a bare apartment.

Bored and antsy, she grabbed the cardboard plate with what was left of its so-called "delectable holiday treat" and carried it into her kitchen alcove. Pulling open the cabinet door under her sink, she jammed the disgusting mess into her trash can. "I could have whipped up a tastier meal out of flour-and-water paste and a crayon."

She turned to her refrigerator and eyed it suspiciously. Dare she open it and forage for more comfort food? She already gained four pounds this month. Giving in to her loneliness and discontent, she pulled open the freezer door. "What's the rule? Feed a fever. Starve a cold. Feed depression huge mounds of ice cream." She grabbed the half-gallon of chunky-minty-fudge, ripped off the lid, tossed it on the kitchen counter and trudged back to the sofa. She kicked off her terry scuffs and put her feet up.

Fluffing a couple of throw pillows she lounged back and settled the tub of ice cream on her belly, her sweatshirt a perfect thermal barrier between her skin and the frigid carton. She grabbed the fork off the TV tray and began digging out forkfuls of chunky-minty-fudge Thanksgiving cheer.

She felt a light thud near her shoulder and knew her kitten, Jaxon, had jumped to the sofa's arm. She reached around and petted the little gray male she rescued last week from behind her Dumpster. So hungry, skinny and pitiful, she couldn't say no. "Hi, baby. So where were you when I needed help eating that delectable turkey slop?"

The kitten meowed as though in response. Kim managed a brief grin. "Yeah? Well, you're out of danger. The evil food has been dispatched to evil food hell." With a finger, she scooped out a tiny amount of the vanilla housing swirls of

mint and fudge chunks, and held it near her shoulder where
the kitten perched. "Have a swig of holiday cheer, Jaxon
honey." She grimaced, wondering for the zillionth time why
she decided to name the kitten after Jax. Why remind herself
on a minute-by-minute basis of the man her heart was supposed to forget?

"Maybe because I need a best buddy, and all my life it's
been Jax. So now that I'm putting him from my mind, you're
my best buddy, and—well, old habits die hard, I guess." *Putting him from your mind? Sure you are.* she scoffed inwardly.
*Like you ever could. You might as well try to live without
breathing.*

She ate ice cream absently, almost angrily, until her head
began to ache. She drilled a knuckle into her temple. "Ouch.
Freezy brain." She jabbed the fork into the ice cream so it
stood up, heaved a sigh and plunked the container on the TV
tray. "Why does my favorite mood lifting ice cream taste like
cardboard and make my brain hurt? Where's the mood lifter
in that?"

Jaxon ambled across her chest, her stomach, onto the sofa,
then leapt nimbly to the wooden TV tray. It wobbled slightly,
but steadied. Kim knew what was on the kitten's mind, but
didn't stop him as he dipped his head into the carton and
began to lick.

"You little pig." She ran her hand along his back. "That's
my comfort food. Yours is over there in the kitchen in that
bowl shaped like a cat's head. Remember? Those perfectly
good, brown rocklike thingies. I'm sure they're yummy."

Deciding her kitten had pigged out enough, she picked up
the container and carried it to the kitchen. The kitten meowed
his objection. "Sorry, little guy, but a good mother does not
allow her kitten to gorge on sweets. It's bad for the hips. Well,
my hips, anyway. It's bad for your teeth."

She dropped the fork into the sink and shoved the ice cream in the freezer. "And, young man," she said, returning to the couch and drawing the kitten onto her lap to pet and cuddle him, "I intend to be a good mother." She grew melancholy. "To you and…" She swallowed hard. How could fate have been so diabolic, to make her pregnant on the one and only— well, four-and-only nights she'd ever lost her sanity and made love without…

She sighed and kissed Jaxon's gray head. "Anyway, you'll be a good first step to learning about mothering and making a little family. You know what? I've never really taken care of anybody other than myself. So it's time I learn to, don't you think? I'm committing myself to caring for you, and then, next year, to my baby."

She could feel the little cat purring through her hands and her breasts. "I know what you're going to say," she went on, as though the kitten weren't falling happily to sleep. "That renting this furniture wasn't very commitment-like. But that's not the same. See, I was a little insane when I came home from Jax's."

She gestured toward the couch. "Which explains the pink furniture." She looked around. Pink chenille tormented her from every angle. "Thank goodness it can go back. But in a way it's been good, since I've had time to study up on what kind of furniture and fabric I should get for a family with a cat and a baby. You see," she said, more quietly, "I've read that you will, from time to time, contribute what is known as a hairball, which I imagine, will pop up while you're on the furniture rather than the kitchen tile or the wood in here. And babies." She stopped. Lord in heaven, she really was going to be a mother. Next July, she would actually give birth to Jax's child. She had moments, flashes, when she felt extreme joy over that knowledge. Then there were moments like this when she felt stark, staring terror.

She shook off her fear of the unknown to concentrate on the kitten. It had been scary bringing the skinny little stranger into her apartment, but now, after only a week, she didn't know what she would do without him. He was so sweet and loving, and just petting him, hearing him purr, helped ease her anxiety.

"Anyway, I understand babies can be every bit as messy as kittens. Hard to believe, but true," she kidded, trying desperately to elevate her mood. "Yes, Mr.-I-Love-To-Unroll-The-Toilet-Paper-And-Shred-It. Apparently babies can be every bit as much work as a kitten." She scrunched down further on the chenille pillows, lying back to stare at the ceiling. "Every bit…" she whispered, her mind trekking away on a well-worn path—back to Jax.

Just how miserably lonely and empty did she have to feel before she started to forget him? Exactly how long did she have to suffer and agonize before the grief of losing him began to soften and melt away? Would she crave the sound of his voice, his laugher, his scent, for months—or years? How much longer would her heart rage with longing to know again the silent moments when they lay in one another's arms, content and at peace? For one more day? Two?

Or forever?

As she stroked the purring kitten, she laid a hand over her belly, not yet rounded with any sign of impending parenthood. Still, she felt genuine, maternal protectiveness for the life growing inside her. A life conceived in lapse and lust.

"No!" she shouted, startling the kitten awake. It meowed and she regretted her outburst. "Sorry, puddin'." She stroked it to calm its momentary agitation. "Mama was wrong." In more ways than just unsettling her kitten. She was shocked by how angry that thought had made her. She knew, when she let herself, that nothing about those nights with Jax, about

making love to him and being loved by him, had anything to do with lapses in judgment or animal lust.

Certainly not on Jax's part. He'd made his love for her clear, again and again. At the time, frighteningly so. True to form, she panicked and ran, her usual modus operandi when dealing with men who displayed a desire for commitment. Except for Perry, who left her before she could leave him.

She'd been so miserable these past weeks, she did the unimaginable. She turned down work, canceled jobs, spiraling down into a pit of self-pity and isolation. It had only been two weeks ago, after having "the flu" for days and days on end— in complete denial about possibly being pregnant—she dragged herself to the doctor. He shocked her back into the world of the living with the truth she had refused to even think—she was pregnant.

Inside her womb a human person—half her and half Jax— slept safely, growing day by day. Suddenly she could feel again, knew hope once more. Life seemed worth living, for a miracle was going on inside her body. A bright and shiny new child was being formed, readied, to be brought into the world.

Her focus became pure and clear. She intended to love this child as well and as tenderly as any child had ever been loved. And she would not be like her mother. This child would have a secure home, a committed parent. There would be no parade of temporary daddies through this child's life.

A tear slid from the corner of her eye to her temple where it melted into her hair. And what of Jax, the baby's father? He had a right to know, didn't he? Of course, she'd pledged never to bother him again, since she knew she had hurt him so many times before. But now they were connected by a child. Should she break her pledge? How messy would contacting him be— if she decided to? How angry was he? How hurt? Had she finally killed off his love for her with her sniveling flight and admonition that he not follow? Would he snarl out his hatred, or would he hop the first plane, want her back, want marriage and family as he had professed in October?

If he did want all that, what would she do? In the cold light of day, was marriage what she wanted? With all she knew about it, the hooks, traps, games, disillusionments and ugly aftermath? If he did show up, what if she succumbed to his charm, which seemed inevitable, considering her present condition. What if, then, after a month or a year, the usual downward cycle began and she started to feel smothered, depressed, irritated by his annoying little traits like... She thought for a moment, struggling to dredge up those traits in her mind. "*Damn*, Jax," she muttered. "Why don't you have any annoying traits? How annoying."

The kitten stirred, repositioned himself to nuzzle his head in the hollow of her throat. His whiskers tickled and she smiled. "Okay, I'll shut up." She wiped away a tear. "But you're going to have to get better at these family discussions. You're not holding up your end. Your lack of advice definitely sucks. I'm in an emotional quagmire. You're my best friend and my shrink, you know." She sniffed. "So, Doc, what do I do about Jax?" she asked.

Her kitten resumed purring, apparently having no intention of helping her with The Jax Problem.

She closed her eyes. "The Jax Problem," she whispered aloud. When she thought she needed healing and consoling about Perry's abandonment, the minute she threw herself into Jax's arms, she was over Perry. She didn't face it right away, allowing herself a few days of self-pity and tissue-tearing, a well established dumpee's privilege. But time revealed the truth. Now she understood her sadness had been battered pride, not the pain of losing someone she loved. She had never loved Perry. But hadn't that been the point? Her relationship mantra was always, "Never get so wrapped up in somebody you can't pick up and leave at a moment's notice."

Without realizing it, and against her will, she smashed that rule to smithereens when she got all wrapped up in loving Jax. All her life she needed him—first, as a friend, then a fortress, and finally, ultimately, as a tender, giving lover.

"I don't blame you for not helping me with The Jax Problem," she murmured, petting Jaxon. "After all, the vet said you're only about ten weeks old. How wise can a kitten be at ten weeks when I'm still flailing around at thirty?" She stroked Jaxon's back for a few more minutes. "I understand, sweetie. What you're saying is you may be Jax's namesake, but loving him too much is my problem."

Loving him too much? Was there such a thing as loving somebody too much? Was that possible, to love somebody too much? *No, you idiot! There is no such problem as loving somebody too much.* She sat up, abruptly, her mind blown with blinding clarity. She set the kitten on the sofa cushion. "Sorry, Jaxon," she said, breathless. "I just had an epiphany. I promise it won't happen often, since this is my first."

The kitten looked at her, stretched, then jumped off the sofa and sauntered toward her bedroom.

"You're right. It'll be quieter in there while the epiphany is going on out here." She jumped up, began to pace. "Okay, since it isn't a terrible curse to love somebody too much, then…" She ran her hands through her hair, concentrating. Somewhere in all her mental turmoil, a quiet voice nudged, *You don't love him too much, Kimberly. You just love him. That's all. It's really quite simple.*

She staggered a step, grasping the wooden mantel above the hearth with both fists. "I just *love* Jax?" she whispered. "I just love Jax," she repeated, this time making a statement of fact. "Not *just* as a friend or *just* as a port in life's storms, or even *just* as a lover, but real love like—two people meant to be together. Two people who like each other, who fight and make up. Who make beautiful love but care about each other as people, happy or sad, sick or well, not merely as sexual objects."

She thought of those elderly couples she saw in the park, holding hands, still in love after-fifty, sixty, even seventy years together. "It's so simple. Why couldn't I see what's been there all my life, so close I didn't notice it until I tried to leave it behind? Only then could I feel the pain of having my life ripped in half."

In the late afternoon silence she could hear her heart battering against her ears. "Jax is my other half," she said, a new fervor in her tone. "He makes me whole. Without him, I'm broken, miserable." She'd heard somewhere that the truth shall set you free—a cliché, because it was so true. With this vital truth finally drawn out of her from a place beyond logic and reason, she felt free, buoyed up.

"I love him like I've never loved anybody, like nobody but Jax has ever loved me. Not my mother, not my father, or any boyfriend I've ever *thought* I cared about, or pretended to care about in my mixed-up, half-baked way. That's the real reason I never committed. Because I already was. But because of my mother's example, I was afraid to understand it." She leaned her forearms on the mantel and covered her face with her hands. "I've been such a stupid, stupid fool!"

The screech of her doorbell shook her. She lifted her head with a jerk and stared at her apartment door. Who could be so rude to be dropping by now—unannounced, on Thanksgiving, in the middle of her life-altering epiphany? *"Go away!"* she shouted, then made a pained face at the magnitude of her stupidity. *Why didn't you just keep quiet, idiot?*

"Open the door, Kimberly."

Her nerves tensed and her heart rate shot up. That voice.

It could be no one else in the world but Jax. She wanted to run to the door, but she couldn't move or respond. She could only stare, wide-eyed and mute.

"Kimberly?" he paused, then said, "I'm not leaving. If you don't open this damn door, I'll kick it in."

The thrill of anticipation skittered along her spine. "K—kick…kick…" she squeaked, all she could get out.

"I'm giving you ten seconds to open this door!" he shouted. "Don't make me break it down!"

Yes, yes, my darling! she cried inwardly. *Break it down!*

Her breath had solidified in her throat, cutting off speech. She was frozen in place, yet infinitely aware, waiting, praying with all her heart and soul, to bear witness to her door splintered into atoms.

He started a booming countdown. "Ten—nine—eight—"

The door blurred with tears, her emotions a tangle of longing and disbelief. Could he really be here, really be ready to bash her door down? She couldn't recall any time when Jax had sounded this angry. But she wasn't afraid. She treasured his anger, honored it, for she knew it was born of love, frustration and need. She understood and welcomed it. *Smash it down,* her heart cried. *I love you, Jax. Not too much, but exactly enough—for forever.*

"Seven—six—five—"

Her tears fell. How ironic that he should come today, the day—almost to the moment—of an awakening that still had her reeling. *Come to me, Jax. Take me in your arms. I won't deny you, or my love for you, ever again.*

"Four—three—two—"

She never heard him shout the number one because the explosive splintering of wood drowned it out. She couldn't imagine ever hearing a sound half so sweet. Her heart filled to overflowing. Jax was here. She couldn't see him clearly through her joyful tears, but there he was—the tall, dark shape amid fragmenting white-painted pine.

She knew when he saw her, for he stilled. She blinked, trying to make him out, to savor the sight of his face. He stood there with battleship solidity, so handsome in black trousers and turtleneck. His sexy bad boy curl lay right where it belonged, tempting and taunting from the center of his forehead. He frowned, not in anger, but concern, as though he didn't break down doors every day and felt some guilt. His dark, watchful eyes held an odd mingling of wary reserve and smoldering passion.

The sight of him standing there so tall, grim and macho-as-hell released her from her paralysis, at least partially. "Hello, Jax," she managed feebly.

His jaw flexed, as though gritting his teeth with resolve. He strode toward her, and she noticed that he limped. "Don't say a word until I've finished what I came here to tell you," he said gruffly.

"Are you hurt?" she asked.

"I may have broken my foot," he said. "Don't talk until—"

"Oh, dear!" Ignoring his command, she grasped his arm and laid it across her shoulders to help support his weight. "Come, sit down. Get off it."

"It's okay. *Damn it,* Kimberly! I have to talk to you."

She led him to the sofa and helped him sit. "Okay, I'm quiet. Go ahead." She sat down next to him, then popped up. "Ice!" She ran into the kitchen, grabbed a dish towel, opened the freezer and pulled out the tray under her ice maker, dumping half the cubes into the towel.

"What in blazes are you doing?" he shouted.

"You need ice on that foot. Take off your shoe and put your leg up on the couch." She gathered the corners of the towel together and hurried back to the sofa. When she saw that he hadn't done as she said, she grasped his leg and lifted it, then pulled off his shoe. When he groaned, she winced. "Sorry." She handed him the towel filled with ice. "Lay this on your foot. It'll keep the swelling down."

"I don't give a flying flip about my foot," he said.

She stood over him, hands on her hips. "Well, I do, so ice it. We're not going any further with this talk until you do." She felt so light, she could almost fly. Jax was here. On her sofa. It seemed miracles really did happen.

He scowled at her, but did as she demanded. "Okay, can I go on?"

She smiled and took a seat on the rug at his feet. "Sure." She gestured broadly. "The floor is yours."

His eyebrows dipped further, as though he expected more resistance.

She nodded her encouragement. She didn't know what he had to say, but a girl could hope. "I'm listening. Talk away."

He shifted his jaw side to side, looking guarded, then began grimly, "I've let you walk out of my life for the last time, Kimberly. I gave you some time. I didn't want to, but I did."

"To keep from strangling me?" she offered.

"What?"

"For the sniveling, cowardly way I walked out on you? You gave me some time so you could cool off, I mean."

He watched her silently for a moment, then waved his hand as though exasperated. "Will you keep the hell quiet for one minute?"

"Sorry," She bit her lip to keep her mouth shut. Having Jax here made her so happy she wanted to talk and talk. It had been so very long. She'd missed him so much.

"No," he said. "The reason I gave you time was to let you find out how much you missed me."

She said nothing, but lifted her eyebrows at his wisdom.

"I've given you all the time I can stomach." He dropped the ice bag, grasped her and pulled her onto his lap. "I'm here now to tell you you're wrong about marriage and commitment. You're so damn wrong, Kimberly, but I don't know how to fix it. I've thought and thought, but I don't know what I can do. I'd cut off an arm if it would make you see that people can stay together. They can fight but they make up. They stick it out even when the hot-and-heavy passion ebbs, because they care about each other, as people, as friends, as human beings, not just sex objects," he said. She relished the heat of their body to body contact, relished the passion in his voice, his eyes. Loved the fact that he was telling her exactly what she'd just told herself. "You knew my parents," he went on. "They had fights, but they never went to bed mad, because they wanted to be together. Damn it, they not only loved each other, they liked each other." He pressed a hand against her cheek, ran his fingers through her hair. "We like each other, don't we?" he asked.

She nodded, swallowing hard as his hand began another tender pass along her temple and through her hair.

"We've fought, but we've made up, haven't we?"

Tears shimmered in her eyes. "Yes," she whispered.

He placed both hands on her cheeks, gently holding her face. "We've made love, and, yes, it's changed our relationship, but it hasn't diminished it, it's only made it whole, made us whole. I feel that so strongly I can't believe that you don't."

A tear slid down her cheek, and he brushed it with his thumb. "Don't cry, Kim. Trust me. Nothing in life is certain. But the way I see it, I'm so miserable, if I'm going to be miserable I'd rather be miserable *with* you than without you." His gaze was intense; his eyes sparkled with emotion. "I honestly don't see us as miserable, as long as we're together. How can I show you, Kimberly? What do you want me to do to prove—"

She placed her fingertips against his lips. "Shush," she said. "Jax, it's not a matter of proving anything," she said.

He grasped her wrist, tugged her hand away from his lips. "Don't say that. Give us a chance. Marry me, and as God is my witness, we'll still be together, still be happy on our fiftieth wedding anniversary."

She ran a finger along the worried crease in his forehead. "Are you allergic to cats?" she asked.

The wild swing of subjects clearly did nothing to ease the worry crease. "What?" He shook his head, at a loss. "What in blazes does that have to do with—"

"Because we have one." She smoothed the errant curl back into the rest of his hair. He smelled so good, just as she remembered. She breathed him in, her happiness billowing.

"We?" he looked unsettled. "Who?"

She realized he thought she referred to some new man in her life and laid both hands on his shoulders in a reassuring gesture. He was so tense. She would have to help him with that. Shaking her head, she said, "We—you and I. We have a cat. Well, he's not quite a cat, yet. He's a kitten, but he's part of my family." She leaned toward him, grazing his lips with her own. "Like you."

When she sat back, she was pleased and a little amused by his expression. He looked as though she'd just told him she loved him or something terrifically monumental like that. Maybe that would be a nice touch to add. Running her hands along his shoulders to his arms she admitted softly, "I love you, Jax. And not just as a friend. I guess I needed these past horrible, lonely weeks to appreciate a truth I've known deep down most of my life."

She snuggled up next to him, laying her cheek against his shoulder. "The truth is, I'm stuck with you for however long it lasts." She kissed his throat. "Whether it's for as many as a hundred years or a paltry sixty or seventy, I'm stuck." She sighed. "And I'm afraid, you are, too."

He shifted her in his arms so that he could see her face, his expression charmingly shocked. She grinned. "It's not as though I didn't enjoy your smashing down my door, though. It was terribly cute."

His brows dipped at her assessment. "Cute?"

"Um hum." She reached up and dragged his bad boy curl down again. She had a sense the sexy bad boy side of him would be a welcome addition to this Thanksgiving day celebration. "I was just about to give you a call, when you showed up."

He looked staggered. "You were?"

"Um hum." She toyed with his curl. "And there's one other thing," she said, secure in his embrace.

He took a deep breath, as though preparing himself.

She skimmed the side of his face with loving fingertips, then slipped her arm under his and around to his back. She hugged him close, struck in that moment by a sense of wholeness, of oneness. She suddenly knew she would never feel alone and broken again, for this man would be there, her tower of strength, her champion, her other half. And she would be all of those things for him. "It's pretty big news. Can you take it?"

His grin was charming, crooked and as welcome as sunshine after a storm. "I can take anything now."

And so could she, she realized. She lifted his hand from where it rested on her thigh and placed it over her belly. "We're pregnant, darling," she whispered, watching his face.

His features registered confusion at first, but an instant later he reacted exactly as she hoped he would, with a whoop of pleasure and a hearty hug. His laughter, deep and rich, tingled through her body. "I can't believe it," he said against her hair. "I never expected to be this happy."

She held him, kissed his throat. "Me, neither, but I think we can learn to tolerate it."

He laughed again, kissed her temple. "I love you so much, Kimberly, it hurts." His kisses trailed along her cheek, nipping, tempting, teasing. The very air around them became charged with electric anticipation. She knew what that meant. Total, utter surrender was seconds away. She pressed her hands against his chest and moved slightly away so she could see his face. "Don't get too frisky, Mr. Macho. Remember, we have no front door."

He glanced at the mess he'd made. "That reminds me. I figured the police would be here by now."

She shook her head. "Neighbors are gone, either out of town or at dinner with relatives."

He grinned, kissed her, murmuring, "Good, then we're alone."

She caught his meaning. "For now, but not for long."

"Why don't we go to a hotel?" He teased her ear with his tongue.

She liked the idea. "It's got to take cats."

He lifted his head to look at her. "Cats?"

"Remember? We have one." She smiled at him. How darling he looked when he was turned on and disoriented. "The whole family goes or nobody goes. It's a commitment thing I'm working on."

He watched her for a long moment, his eyes glistening with love. Then he kissed the tip of her nose. "Of course the cat goes with us."

She had a thought. "How's your foot?"

"What foot?" His fingers traced the line of her cheekbone.

She laughed. "Your broken foot."

"It's great," he said, his mind clearly on other things.

She pushed away, scooting off his lap. "Is it really great or is it broken?" She stood, retrieved the towel and its melting ice. "If it's broken we need to get you to an emergency room."

He took her hand. "It's just bruised." Pulling her back into his lap, he nipped at her ear, sending a thrill coursing through her. "Pack up the cat, sweetheart. I'll call a door repairman."

"On Thanksgiving?"

He smiled, glancing around at her living room. "I guess it can wait till tomorrow. This pink furniture is safe enough."

She pretended to be affronted. "You don't like it?"

He kissed her knuckles and she felt all hot and melty in the pit of her stomach. "I love it," he whispered. "Every screaming piece.

"It's rented."

"Thank God."

She giggled. "You might write a note to tape outside the broken door giving the number of the hotel, so the landlord knows I'm okay."

"Okay, now get *our* cat before we forget ourselves and do something discriminating couples usually try not to do in public."

She threw her arms around his neck and kissed him hard, then darted away before she lost her mind completely. "I'll be right back with Jaxon."

"Jaxon?"

She paused at the bedroom door and shrugged sheepishly. "I needed a best friend, didn't I?" She inclined her head toward the bedroom. "He's young. He can get used to a new name. What do you think about Spike?"

"I'm crazy about it." Jax's smile filled her with a delicious glow. It took all her will power not to rush back into his arms and make wild, crazy love to him right there on her ugly pink chenille in front of God and anybody who might pass in the hall.

Yes, she thought, *I have a lot to be thankful for—my kitty, our baby, and the most blessed gift of all—my darling Jax.*

HARLEQUIN ROMANCE

From sexy bosses to surprise babies— these ladies have got everyone talking!

Keely, Emma and Tahlia work together at a small, trendy design company in Melbourne. They've become the best of friends, meeting for breakfast, chatting over a midmorning coffee and a doughnut—or going for a cocktail after work. They've loved being single in the city…but now three gorgeous new men are about to enter their work lives, transform their love lives— and give them loads more to gossip about!

First, we meet Keely in…

IMPOSSIBLY PREGNANT
by Nicola Marsh (#3866)

A positive pregnancy test is a surprise for Keely!

On-sale October 2005

THE SHOCK ENGAGEMENT
by Ally Blake (#3870)

On-sale November 2005

TAKING ON THE BOSS
by Darcy Maguire (#3874)

On-sale December 2005

Available wherever Harlequin books are sold.

www.eHarlequin.com

HROG

HARLEQUIN ROMANCE®

**This November Harlequin Romance®
brings you two entertaining, brand-new
short stories in one volume....**

SECRET CHATS AT THE WATER COOLER,
STOLEN MOMENTS IN THE STATIONERY
CUPBOARD—THESE COUPLES ARE FINDING
IT'S IMPOSSIBLE TO KEEP THINGS...

STRICTLY BUSINESS!

The Temp and the Tycoon
Liz Fielding

After a disastrous first day Tallie's sure her hot new boss,
Jude Radcliffe, will hate her forever—they're complete
opposites! Jude is married to his work, and Tallie, well, she
thinks life is for living! But Tallie has decided her real job will
be to persuade Jude to live life to the max—with her!

The Fiancé Deal
Hannah Bernard

Louise Henderson might be fighting for the same promotion
as sexy lawyer David Tyler, but she's in a bind, she needs a
fiancé fast—and David's the man for the job! But now Lou has
just discovered she's won the coveted promotion! Will the man
she's fallen in love with be happy—now she's the boss...?

#3868 On sale November 2005

Available wherever Harlequin books are sold.

www.eHarlequin.com

HRSB

If you enjoyed what you just read,
then we've got an offer you can't resist!

Take 2 bestselling love stories FREE!

Plus get a FREE surprise gift!

Clip this page and mail it to Harlequin Reader Service®

IN U.S.A.	IN CANADA
3010 Walden Ave.	P.O. Box 609
P.O. Box 1867	Fort Erie, Ontario
Buffalo, N.Y. 14240-1867	L2A 5X3

YES! Please send me 2 free Harlequin Romance® novels and my free surprise gift. After receiving them, if I don't wish to receive anymore, I can return the shipping statement marked cancel. If I don't cancel, I will receive 6 brand-new novels every month, before they're available in stores! In the U.S.A., bill me at the bargain price of $3.57 plus 25¢ shipping & handling per book and applicable sales tax, if any*. In Canada, bill me at the bargain price of $4.05 plus 25¢ shipping & handling per book and applicable taxes**. That's the complete price and a savings of 10% off the cover prices—what a great deal! I understand that accepting the 2 free books and gift places me under no obligation ever to buy any books. I can always return a shipment and cancel at any time. Even if I never buy another book from Harlequin, the 2 free books and gift are mine to keep forever.

186 HDN DZ72
386 HDN DZ73

Name	(PLEASE PRINT)	
Address	Apt.#	
City	State/Prov.	Zip/Postal Code

Not valid to current Harlequin Romance® subscribers.
Want to try another series? Call 1-800-873-8635
or visit www.morefreebooks.com.

* Terms and prices subject to change without notice. Sales tax applicable in N.Y.
** Canadian residents will be charged applicable provincial taxes and GST.
 All orders subject to approval. Offer limited to one per household.
 ® are registered trademarks owned and used by the trademark owner and or its licensee.

HROM04R   ©2004 Harlequin Enterprises Limited

eHARLEQUIN.com

The Ultimate Destination for Women's Fiction

For **FREE online reading,** visit
www.eHarlequin.com now and enjoy:

Online Reads
Read **Daily** and **Weekly** chapters from
our Internet-exclusive stories by your
favorite authors.

Interactive Novels
Cast your vote to help decide how these
stories unfold...then stay tuned!

Quick Reads
For shorter romantic reads, try our
collection of Poems, Toasts, & More!

Online Read Library
Miss one of our online reads?
Come here to catch up!

Reading Groups
Discuss, share and rave with other
community members!

For great reading online,
visit www.eHarlequin.com today!

INTONL04R

SILHOUETTE *Romance*®

*S*hakespeare in Love

Timeless classics lead to modern love!

**Don't miss one scene of
Silhouette Romance's newest production.**

Much Ado About Matchmaking
by MYRNA MACKENZIE
SR 1786

Taming of the Two
by ELIZABETH HARBISON
SR 1790

Twelfth Night Proposal
by KAREN ROSE SMITH
SR 1794

Only from Silhouette Books!

Visit Silhouette Books at www.eHarlequin.com   SRMAAM

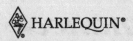

HARLEQUIN®

HARLEQUIN ROMANCE®

Coming Next Month

#3867 THEIR NEW-FOUND FAMILY Rebecca Winters

As a single mom, Rachel Marsden has always tried to do her best by her daughter. So when Natalie's long-lost father, Tris Monbrisson, shows up Rachel swallows her feelings. For the summer they will move to Tris's beautiful home in the mountains of Switzerland. But as she and Tris fall into the role of mother and father, the secrets of the past unravel....

#3868 STRICTLY BUSINESS Liz Fielding and Hannah Bernard (2 stories in 1 volume)

The Temp and the Tycoon by Liz Fielding—Her new boss, Jude Radcliff, is all work and no play...can Tallie persuade him to live life to the max—with her...?

The Fiancé Deal by Hannah Bernard—Louise Henderson is fighting for the same promotion as sexy lawyer David Tyler. She needs a fiancé fast—and David's the best man for the job!

#3869 MISTLETOE MARRIAGE Jessica Hart

For Sophie Beckwith, this Christmas means facing the ex who dumped her and then married her sister! Only one person can help: her best friend Bram. Bram used to be engaged to Sophie's sister, and now, determined to show the lovebirds that they've moved on, he's come up with a plan: he's proposed to Sophie!

#3870 THE SHOCK ENGAGEMENT by Ally Blake

Emma's colleagues and friends are delighted she is marrying the gorgeous and successful dot com millionaire Harry Buchanan—but their engagement is purely for convenience. Harry will get out of the excruciating "hunkiest male" competition and Emma will save her job. Only, Emma has dreamed of marrying Harry for years, and acting engaged is pure torture....

Office Gossip